'I don't know how I've kept my hands off you,' he murmured, as his lips found the tender skin below her ear. 'You don't know what you do to me, Folly. Or perhaps you do.'

The words caressed her, teased her. 'Perhaps you feel the same. . .' His cheek was rough against the smoothness of her skin. 'I think you do, Folly. Don't you?'

His expert hands. . . Yes, that was it. Luke was an expert lover in every sense. He knew exactly how to touch her—how to stir her. But how had he learned that expertise? In other women's arms. . . She thought of Cherith, and the creator of the fire-tapestries. And the woman on the phone. No doubt they had all felt this melting ecstacy. . . And now it was her turn. But for how long?

WE HOPE you're enjoying our new addition to our Contemporary Romance Series—stories which take a light-hearted look at the Zodiac and show that love can be written in the stars!

Every month you can get to know a different combination of star-crossed lovers, with one story that follows the fortunes of a hero and heroine when they embark on the romance of a lifetime with somebody born under another sign of the Zodiac. This month features a sizzling love-affair between **Aries** and **Leo**.

To find out more fascinating facts about this month's featured star sign, turn to the back pages of this book...

Eleanor Rees says: 'I was delighted when my editor asked me to write a StarSign Romance, because I have always been interested in astrology. In fact, I actually studied it quite seriously at one time, and took an examination with a view to taking it up professionally. But that was before my first romance was accepted... Since then, I haven't had time for anything but writing.

My star sign is Libra, which is a very romantic sign. Love is as essential to us as air to breath—and that's what writing for Mills & Boon is all about.'

HUNTER'S HAREM

BY

ELEANOR REES

MILLS & BOON LIMITED
ETON HOUSE 18–24 PARADISE ROAD
RICHMOND SURREY TW9 1SR

All the characters in this book have no existence outside the imagination of the Author, and have no relation whatsoever to anyone bearing the same name or names. They are not even distantly inspired by any individual known or unknown to the Author, and all the incidents are pure invention.

All Rights Reserved. The text of this publication or any part thereof may not be reproduced or transmitted in any form or by any means, electronic or mechanical, including photocopying, recording, storage in an information retrieval system, or otherwise, without the written permission of the publisher.

This book is sold subject to the condition that it shall not, by way of trade or otherwise, be lent, resold, hired out or otherwise circulated without the prior consent of the publisher in any form of binding or cover other than that in which it is published and without a similar condition including this condition being imposed on the subsequent purchaser.

First published in Great Britain 1992 by Mills & Boon Limited

© Eleanor Rees 1992

*Australian copyright 1992
Philippine copyright 1992
This edition 1992*

ISBN 0 263 77478 3

STARSIGN ROMANCES is a trademark of Harlequin Enterprises B.V., Fribourg Branch. Mills and Boon is an authorised user.

*Set in 10 on 11½ pt Linotron Times
01-9203-55315 Z
Typeset in Great Britain by Centracet, Cambridge
Made and printed in Great Britain*

CHAPTER ONE

APHROSYNE TAYLOR-AGATHANGELOU, now more commonly known as Folly Taylor, emerged from the Rose Bowl—from *her* Rose Bowl—in a daze of excited speculation. At last she was in London — and with a business of her own!

The possibilities were endless. 'Certainly, your Highness,' she bobbed in her mind's eye. 'I would be delighted to design the flowers for your wedding. . . ' The daydream was so engrossing that she almost didn't see the man and the girl struggling on the pavement opposite. But just then one of the girl's flailing blows hit home, and the man swore savagely in a deep, and somehow unforgettable voice.

His harsh words jerked Folly out of her fantasy and back to the real world. A world where the man with the voice was apparently attacking a woman much slighter and younger than himself—and, despite the victim's blonde prettiness, none of the passers-by on the busy little London street was making the slightest attempt to stop him.

The warning her anxious mother had impressed on her as they'd waited for Folly's plane at Athens airport had obviously been quite correct. Londoners *were* more callous than the Greeks she had grown up with. Well, she might be half-English herself, but there was no way *she* could just stand by and watch. Seizing a bunch of roses from the display outside the Rose Bowl's window, Folly launched herself across the street.

Only when she was halfway there did she remember that this, after all, wasn't Chipchester, where she had spent the last six months at college—nor even Athens, where at least the drivers and pedestrians expected to engage in constant warfare—and that perhaps she should have checked the traffic before crossing. . .

But, fortunately for her future royal customers, the narrow street outside the shop was free of traffic. She reached the other side unscathed just as the man gave a grunt of triumph and twisted his victim's hand behind her back, wrenching what looked like a purse out of her hand.

'Leave her alone, you brute!' Folly lashed the aggressor over the head with her roses—which immediately disintegrated in a hail of scented petals. The man ignored her, and she cursed the professional thoroughness that had led the florist to de-thorn the blooms. Then she realised that her other hand held a much more potent weapon.

Dropping the useless stems, she used all her strength to swing her briefcase in a wide arc, bringing it crashing into the man's stomach. The locks burst open, spilling her newly signed lease on to the dusty pavement, but the other results of the blow were equally immediate—and satisfactorily dramatic. There was an 'Oof!' of expelled air as the man fell to his knees, his broad shoulders heaving as he strained for his next breath.

His victim took one disbelieving look at her unlikely rescuer and then, before Folly could reassure her, the girl had turned tail and was running nimbly down the street. Within seconds, her blonde head was lost in the crowds.

Only then did Folly realise that she had left her purse behind. More of a wallet than a purse, it still lay where the man had dropped it. Folly stooped quickly and picked it up. With luck, it would contain enough information to trace its owner.

She was just about to investigate when a long, shuddering breath from the man at her feet reminded her that it might be as well to remove herself from the scene before the winded assailant recovered enough to take his revenge. It went against the grain to let the brute escape scot-free, but, with his victim disappeared, there seemed no point in calling the police.

And now she took a better look at him, Folly couldn't help noticing the strong, muscular lines of the broad back under that white shirt. And, even with the man still on his knees and half doubled-up with pain, his head, with its swept-back mane of hair, was still at a level with her waist. . . Recovered, he might be a formidable opponent. She started to back away.

'Oh, no, you don't, miss.' To Folly's surprise, the voice came not from the stranger, but from somewhere behind and above her. Her gaze fixed on her adversary, she had backed straight into what felt rather like a human version of the Great Wall of China. She looked round and noticed that this particular edifice seemed to be dressed in dark blue. . . One large, official hand grasped her by the elbow.

'Now, perhaps you'd like to tell me what you're doing with this gentleman's wallet?'

'What?' For a moment, Folly was taken aback, but then she realised that the policeman had probably only seen the last few seconds of their little drama. 'Oh, no—it's not his wallet.'

She laughed a little nervously, unable to help noticing out of the corner of her eye that the little crowd which had gathered was melting rapidly away now that official help had arrived. She felt a qualm of doubt. Was she going to be left as the only witness? Why did she have to get herself mixed up in a thing like this on her first day in London? But at least she was safe from the man on the ground, who now seemed to be recovering and was looking up at her with intense fury as he rubbed the area just below his ribs. 'He stole it from a girl,' she explained quickly, before she could feel intimidated. 'I saw him attack her——'

'She's lying, officer.' The voice purred with a fury that made it no less memorable. Even in anger, it was rich and deep—with a tone of natural authority that made the policeman behind her tense involuntarily, as if he had to fight an urge to stand to attention.

As the man unfolded his tall frame and stood up, slinging a dusty jacket over one broad shoulder, Folly realised how right she had been to see him as formidable. He was as tall as the Great Wall behind her, but with a lean solidity that was every bit as impressive as the policeman's sheer bulk.

It also began to occur to her that he was very well dressed for a pickpocket—but no doubt the streets of central London provided rich pickings. And a respectable exterior would be part of the thief's stock-in-trade.

His eyes narrowed as he looked at her, and seemed to glow with fury, their brown tint lightening almost to gold. 'She and the other girl were obviously in league,' he went on with savage certainty. 'The blonde picked my pocket and then when I grabbed her this one came rushing up and knocked the breath out of me. If you hadn't come along with you did she'd have been off with my wallet and no doubt they'd split the pickings later.'

Folly listened in disbelief. 'But that's rubbish. . .'

'Is it?' The man turned away from her dismissively, and back to the policeman. 'Don't let's waste time,

Constable. There's a perfectly simple method of proving this. My credit cards will have my name on them.'

'And that is, sir?' The policeman seemed to be treating him with far too much respect, Folly thought with irritation. Almost as if he believed his story. . . And she herself started to feel another niggle of doubt. He did sound so very sure of himself—and, now that she came to look at it, the wallet she was handing over so meekly did have a distinctly masculine air. . .

'Luke Hunter.' The man's voice was grimly confident.

Luke Hunter. . .Why did that name seem familiar? And more importantly, if it weren't his wallet would he have dared to give his name?

'Luke Hunter.' The constable shuffled through the wallet's contents, and read the name from what appeared to be a discreetly platinum-coloured card. For a few seconds Folly's vivid imagination conjured up a fantasy in which the girl she had rescued had been named by a father desperate for a son . . .Or perhaps 'Luke' might be short for Lucia?

But by the time the policeman had slipped the imposing piece of plastic back into its place and handed the wallet over with a ponderous, 'That seems to be in order, sir,' she had accepted the truth.

And almost at the same moment she remembered why the name 'Luke Hunter' was so familiar. Only ten minutes before, the current owner of the Rose Bowl, the rather oppressively genteel Miss Philimore, had been telling her about the wealthy local businessman who was one of the Rose Bowl's best customers. . .

'Oh, Lord,' she said weakly, looking at the blank hostility on the two male faces before her. 'I seem to have done it again.'

'Again? You mean you make a habit of this kind of

thing? I hope you're taking all this down, Constable.' Such was the power of Luke Hunter's voice that Folly saw the policeman reach automatically towards his breast pocket and take out a notebook.

Folly realised that the situation was slipping out of her control. That stupid man—— But if only she could explain before the policeman took official note of what had happened, the situation might remain relatively simple... 'It was a perfectly natural mistake, Mr Hunter. I thought *you* were attacking *her*, you see.'

'I'm not sure I do.' The man was brushing the London dust from his dark-suited legs, and she couldn't see his face. 'Do I look like the sort of man who makes his living attacking women?' His anger was under control now, and his voice was lazily mocking.

'No—no, of course not.' He obviously didn't plan to make it easy for her. 'I'm sorry,' she apologised stiffly. 'And I'm sorry I hit you, too. But you've got your wallet back, so there's really no harm done, is there?' She turned back to the constable. 'I'm sure Mr Hunter understands.'

For a moment she thought all was well. The policeman's vast bulk relaxed visibly. 'Well, miss——' he started. But before the notebook could begin its return journey Luke Hunter's mocking tones cut in again.

'I hardly think this is the place to be discussing this, Constable. No doubt you have the proper facilities for taking statements down at the station.'

It took a moment or two for what he was saying to sink in. 'Down at the station? But that's ridiculous!'

The constable looked at Luke's implacable face, then at the growing crowd that was beginning to re-group. 'I think it might be better, miss,' he said uncertainly. 'Perhaps you'd better follow me...'

* * *

'Honestly, Mum—I thought I was never going to get away. And the infuriating thing was, I'm sure that horrible man believed me long before he admitted it. It was as if he was deliberately stringing it out.'

At the other end of the international line, Mrs Agathangelou sounded only mildly surprised by the tale of the afternoon's adventures. She had long since grown used to the sight of her only daughter charging recklessly into battle—usually with her hand firmly clasped on the wrong end of the stick.

'Well, I expect he was annoyed, dear,' she said judiciously. 'You did hit him in the stomach—and that briefcase of yours is quite a solid design, after all. Those metal corners. . . Besides, he probably felt that he'd been made to look foolish, and men do hate that. It was rather your own fault, Folly, dear. You do tend to rush into things. It's what comes of being an Aries, I suppose. And if he's a fire-sign too, like Leo or Sagittarius, it would explain why sparks fly when you get together.'

But Folly was in no mood to have her character analysed—and she knew that once her mother started on her favourite hobby-horse she was quite capable for going on for hours. 'If you ask me, Mum, he was born under the Sign of the Pig. I mean, what else was I supposed to do? I didn't know that girl was a pickpocket. As far as I was concerned, Mr Luke Beastly Hunter was attacking her, not the other way round.'

She still felt aggrieved to think how long it had taken to persuade the police of that simple fact. Luke Hunter was the sort of man who rode roughshod over everyone else's opinions—if she had been there alone she was sure she could have convinced them in a fraction of the time.

'After all,' she went on, 'I had a perfectly valid reason for being there. It was right outside the Rose

Bowl, and I had the lease and everything in my briefcase.'

'Well, that was good, dear. At least you could prove who you were.'

'Don't you believe it!' Folly could feel her hackles rise all over again. 'They were very sniffy about me giving my address as this hotel. And then Mr Clever-Clogs Hunter spotted that the name on the lease wasn't the same as the one I'd given—Aphrosyne rather than Folly, of course, and the surnames all in full, whereas normally I just use "Taylor" over here, to save spelling it out. But the policeman wouldn't even have noticed, if you ask me. So then they have to fill out all the forms all over again and I get a stern warning against giving false information to police officers! Oh!'

She took a deep breath and tried to calm down. 'The whole thing was a perfectly natural mistake, but, thanks to him, they went on as if I'd just attempted to rob the Bank of England. Taking statements and everything. . . And then at last that—that *man* just announces that he has decided not to press charges. And off he goes. Smiling.'

She remembered that smile with resentful clarity. It hadn't been a particularly nice smile. There had been something predatory about it; the sort of smile a fox might give the remaining chickens when he left the hen-house. Or, rather, a lion—there was something about those gold-brown eyes and swept-back mane of hair that made her think of the King of Beasts, dressed up in the trappings of civilisation. Luke Hunter. . .His name suited him. But what—or who—was his prey?

She had had an unpleasant feeling it might have been her. 'That's it for the moment,' his smile seemed to say. 'But I'll be back.' And he had called her by her full Greek name too, as if to remind her that he knew it. That he could find her whenever he chose. . .

But that was ridiculous. Folly shivered. Luke Hunter would probably run a mile rather than meet her again. Two miles if he had any sense. Oh, why did she never meet any *nice* men?

Her mother must have heard her sigh. 'There's nothing else the matter, is there, darling?' she queried at once, breaking off her own remarks. 'Nothing went wrong about the lease?'

'Oh, no—that was all fine. Signed and sealed—I know you said to have a solicitor check it over first, but there were some other people after it, and there didn't seem any point waiting.'

'Oh, but——'

Folly grinned to herself. Her mother was a born worrier. 'Don't worry,' she said soothingly. 'It's a super little shop, Mum—just what I wanted. It would have been madness to lose it. I actually take possession in about a month, but as soon as I've found a flat I'm going to start working there part-time to learn the ropes. The owner's a Miss Philimore—I didn't much like her, but she seems helpful enough. And the girl that works there wants to stay on. . .'

She could hear the doubt in her own voice as she remembered the gum-chewing, spiky-haired teenager whom she had seen watering the plants. 'Though I'm not too sure about her. She seems a bit couldn't-careless. But Miss Philimore seems to think she's all right so long as she's watched, and it would save me having to look for someone else.'

'So it's all working out beautifully.' Folly could almost hear the expansive gesture as her mother manfully swallowed her doubts. Her acquired accent sounded suddenly very strong. Despite Mrs

Agathangelou's determination to remain English, the twenty-three years she had spent in Greece had left their mark. 'So why the sighs?'

Folly smiled. The older woman might be over a thousand miles away, but there was nothing wrong with her hearing. Or her instincts. 'Oh, I was just thinking what a pity it is that all good-looking men are such beasts,' she said, with more real feeling than she intended.

'Now, darling, don't be cynical.' Her mother sounded concerned. 'Just because that dreadful Tony——'

'Oh, bother Tony. I wasn't thinking about him.' Folly realised with a stab of surprise that that was actually true. 'Though he illustrates my point. But it was the Hunter man I was talking about.'

'He was good-looking, then?'

'Oh, very.' She laughed at the speculative tone that her mother couldn't quite hide. 'About thirty-four, I suppose—and terribly English, if you know what I mean. Though he did have a bit of a tan, unlike most of the men over here. Brown, wavy hair—not that really *dark* brown, but the sort that goes lighter in the sun. And the most extraordinary eyes.' She shivered as she remembered the way they had seemed almost to change colour from darkest brown to angry almost-gold. 'Tall, too,' she remembered. 'Well over six feet, I think he must have been——'

Folly broke off, suddenly aware that the detail of her description was unlikely to allay her mother's suspicions. 'Look, Mum, I just spent most of the afternoon staring at the man—but in fury, not admiration. As far as I'm concerned, after the fiasco with Tony, I've lost interest in romance. And besides, I won't have time. The Rose Bowl is going to take all my energies from now on.'

'I suppose so, dear.' Her mother's gentle voice didn't sound particularly convinced. 'And I know you like your independence. But you mustn't judge all the men you meet by that dreadful Tony. After all, I don't know what I'd do without your father.'

'You and Papa are the exception that proves the rule, darling,' Folly said fondly. 'The one-in-a-million chance—a holiday romance that really worked. You can hardly expect lightning to strike twice in the same family.'

But although she recognised the truth of what she was saying, Folly felt suddenly depressed. At some unconscious level that was exactly what she *had* expected six months earlier—to step off the plane and see the man of her dreams waiting for her on the tarmac. Just as her mother had done when she'd arrived in Athens so many years before.

Seen through her mother's eyes, far-off England had seemed a land of dreams and adventure. And especially romance. No wonder Folly had been so sure that Tony was the one. . .

Resolutely she stamped out that thought. 'Look, we mustn't get on to chattering about your lurid past. Give my love to Papa. I don't know how much this call is costing, and I must get up early tomorrow. I need to start flat-hunting in earnest now that the lease is signed.'

They said their goodbyes. Folly put the phone down and sat on the bed, looking round the poky little hotel room that was all she could afford while she searched for more permanent accommodation. But rather to her surprise, the expected wave of self-pity didn't come.

'I wasn't thinking about Tony. . .' she had said to her mother. And it had been the truth. For the first time in weeks the thought of her broken engagement hadn't been lurking to ambush her.

Perhaps the change of scene was working after all, she thought as she started to strip off her clothes and prepare for bed. And the excitement of her new venture... In less than a month the Rose Bowl would be hers. Her own business! The independence she had always longed for would be hers at last. There would be no time to worry about Tony, or anything—or anyone—else.

She would think about nothing but work.

Starting from now.

Folly slipped between the sheets and closed her eyes with resolution. But it wasn't Tony's image that slipped past her defences and into her dreams.

It was a tall Englishman with mocking brown eyes and a lazy predatory smile. And it wasn't self-pity that kept her tossing and turning till dawn...

CHAPTER TWO

'FLOWERS? Why should anyone be sending me flowers?' Folly pushed herself reluctantly up in bed and attempted to wipe the sleep from her eyes.

The maid who had woken her stared back without comprehension or interest. 'Flowers,' she said again. Folly realised that it was probably the only relevant English word she knew. She had chosen the hotel for its low prices rather than its almost non-existent amenities, so she was rather surprised to find that they had a maid at all. It would have been too much to hope for one capable of answering any of the questions that were beginning to raise their heads in her sleep-muffled brain.

Like, who knew she was here? She hadn't even known herself where she would be staying until she had walked out of the station the day before and asked a taxi-driver to take her somewhere clean and as cheap as possible. So how could anyone be sending her flowers?

But the girl was still standing expectantly in the centre of the room, the bouquet cradled in her arms. It dawned on Folly that she was waiting for a tip and, gathering what she could of her wits, she struggled out of bed to delve in her handbag.

This was plainly an international language. The maid's vacant expression was replaced momentarily by one of greedy expectation—shortly followed by disappointment. She stared with disdain at the coin Folly had given her and almost threw the flowers on to the bed before flouncing out of the room.

With automatic professionalism Folly had carried them into the bathroom and begun to hunt around for a suitable container before her mind turned back to the question of who could have sent them.

She ticked off the possibilities in her mind. None of her college friends knew where she was staying, or would have been the slightest bit likely to make such a gesture, even if they had. Her mother, on the other hand, had been told her address the night before—but it seemed highly unlikely that Mrs Agathangelou would have splashed out on such an opulent bouquet to welcome her daughter to London.

Folly's practised eye assessed the hothouse blooms in their crackling cellophane wrapper. At a conservative estimate they had cost considerably more than she had just paid for her night's lodging. And her parents' small hotel had always kept them comfortable, rather than wealthy. Even with one less mouth to feed, her mother would hardly be so extravagant.

No, it couldn't be her mother. Nor was it likely to be the proprietress of the Rose Bowl celebrating their deal. Miss Philimore had behaved pleasantly enough, but there had been a calculating set to her narrow mouth that made such a gesture seem unlikely in the extreme.

And as far as Folly could remember, there had been no reason to mention the name of the hotel to anyone else—except, of course, the police constable who had taken down her details. She grinned to herself. Her mother had always impressed on her how wonderful the British policemen were, but this would be politeness beyond the call of duty. . .

And then her heart almost stopped as she remembered—and wondered instantly how she could ever have forgotten. There was one other man who knew where to find her. A man who had stood there smiling at her discomfiture. The same man whose golden-brown eyes had tormented her dreams. . .

Luke Hunter.

Folly flew back into the tiny bathroom and tore at the wide satin ribbon which bound the base of the cellophane package. And yes—underneath, there was a card. Addressed with every name she possessed. And as she pulled it out from between the stems the little rose-bowl motif in the corner of the envelope seemed to spring out at her, drying her mouth in trepidation.

'One of our best customers. . .' Miss Philimore's self-satisfied tones came back to her as she fumbled with the tiny envelope. She wasn't quite sure why the possibility that it was Luke Hunter who had sent her the flowers was so disturbing. . . After all, she would certainly have agreed that an apology was in order.

The trouble was that it seemed as likely as a lion apologising to a gazelle. Mr Hunter hadn't struck her as a man who would easily admit he was wrong. Somehow she felt certain that he would always be far too sure of himself even to consider the possibility.

So why was her heart beating so wildly as she pulled out the card, as if its message was somehow important? It was ridiculous. With a gesture of impatience, Folly forced herself to read it.

Or at least she tried. For a few moments her still-sleepy eyes refused to focus on the dramatic black handwriting. And even when it became clearer—in a purely physical sense—as far as understanding it went she was as far from clarity as ever.

The little card bore one single, short sentence.

'To err is human. . .'

And that was all. It was unsigned. But somehow Folly could only think of one person who might have sent her so tantalising a message.

The words hovered on the edge of Folly's consciousness for the rest of the day as she plodded with increasing grimness from one unsuitable or unaffordable flat to another. What had Luke Hunter meant—if indeed he had been the sender? Though who else could it be? And was his cryptic message supposed to imply forgiveness for her own error—or some kind of apology for his own?

If the second, it was gratifying; if the first, merely infuriating. But in either case, why had he bothered? There seemed no point, unless it was just a question of wanting to get the last word. But in that case, why not sign his name? He couldn't know how few people there were who might be expected to send her flowers. For all Luke Hunter knew, she might have put his gesture down to quite another source.

It could so easily have happened. Two months earlier she would have assumed they came from Tony. And he, with his aptitude for deceit, would no doubt have accepted her gratitude willingly, however undeserved. As he had accepted her love. . .

For a moment the memories came sweeping back. That was what had hurt most, the memory of her naïvete. And the fact that none of her so-called friends at the college—not even her room-mate—had cared enough to warn her that her handsome fiancé apparently regarded an engagement as no pressing reason to stop 'playing the field'. . .

As she stared unseeingly at the advertisements in yet

another newsagent's window Folly felt the old anger come surging back. They had all known; that was the awful thing. For months it had apparently been common knowledge; something to be tutted over and discussed in hushed tones that stopped abruptly whenever she entered the common-room. He had even made passes at some of her fellow students. But, encased in the false security of her new-found happiness, she had never guessed. And not one person had been kind enough—or loyal enough—to tell her the truth.

Eventually she had found out about it in the worst possible way. Finding herself passing Tony's lodgings one evening when they'd had no pre-arranged date, she had decided on impulse to drop in and surprise him.

It had certainly been a surprise. Not just for Tony, but for Folly as well—and for the other girl. The one who was sharing Tony's bed—and sharing it so enthusiastically that neither of them heard Folly's approaching footsteps until she walked right into the room.

Oh, he had come out with all the usual male excuses. That it 'wasn't important'—that it had 'meant nothing'—that he still loved her. He had even had the gall to blame it on Folly herself; to say it would never have happened if she had been more 'reasonable'. Less of a prude.

If she had slept with him, he had meant, and agreed to move in with him as he had wanted. But, confident in her expectation that they would soon be married, Folly had been determined to wait.

She had been so certain then that 'love' would mean 'forever'. Of course, she had known that more unofficial arrangements were common enough in England. But in the society where she had been brought up marriage was still very much the expected norm.

Although the waiting had been difficult, she had wanted everything to be perfect—and she had thought Tony had understood.

Evidently she had been wrong. She still went cold inside when she remembered the things he'd said. She had just stood there, scarcely able to breathe, and aware that only a hair's breadth of control separated her from a fury that would shake her to her soul. And then the girl had giggled, in what Folly now realised was probably a nervous reaction. And that had been it.

The fire-ball of anger inside her had flared into life, and she had flown at him, screaming—what, she could hardly remember, except that more than half of it had been in Greek. And that she had made it perfectly clear that, to her, fidelity and trust meant more than just nothing—meant everything, in fact. And that she would never settle for anything less.

It had ended with Tony manhandling her out of the house. And the tidal wave of emotion had left her drained for days.

Yes, it had been the worst possible way to discover his betrayal. And, since her friends had known, but still let her walk right into it, Folly had decided impulsively that they weren't friends at all, and changed her plans.

Instead of completing her college course, she would draw on the money her English grandmother had left her and go straight into business for herself. As far away from Chipchester as possible. So when the advert for the Rose Bowl had appeared in the trade Press it had seemed like an answer to a prayer.

So here she was. She had made a big mistake, but now it was over. 'To err is human'. . . And it was all working out.

So why did she suddenly feel so close to tears?

Because she was tired of looking at flats that were really bedsits, and bedsits that were really cupboards, but cost as much as if they had been flats. Because the queues at the sandwich bar had been so horrendous that she had decided to go without lunch and now she was feeling disconnected and light-headed. Because it was beginning to rain.

And because, somehow, Luke Hunter had caught her off balance with his flowers and cryptic messages. He had jolted open a door in her mind that she had been keeping carefully shut. Well, perhaps that was all to the good. It couldn't stay closed forever. Perhaps it was time to begin remembering. Perhaps then she could start to forget.

Folly felt suddenly bone tired. It would have to be a taxi back to the hotel—she couldn't afford it, but she knew that the London Tube system would be unbearable, with the rush-hour well into its stride. Would she ever feel at home in this relentless, pitiless city? It wasn't the bustling energy she objected to, but the impersonality. Athens had been hot and noisy, but it had had a human heart. The people had been friendly, and she had known her way around. Here, she felt she would always be an outsider. Had it all been another mistake?

But the lease was signed. If it was a mistake she was committed to it now. And from somewhere inside she felt a spurt of rebellious determination.

'I'll make it work. I *will*. . .' And then a taxi stopped at her frantic signalling, and she was collapsing on to the slippery leather seat with a surge of relief that banished all other thoughts from her mind. Even Luke Hunter. For a while.

* * *

The next day was the same. *Exactly* the same. Except that this time the note said,

'To forgive, divine. . .'

and she had to ask Reception for another vase because the first one was full up. And she caught the bus home instead of another expensive taxi. But, apart from that, the only flats she could see were still as small and impossibly expensive. And she still didn't know what was on Luke Hunter's mind.

But the day after that things began to get a little clearer. This time Reception said they had run out of vases and, whatever he'd done, didn't she think it was time she forgave him? And the note said,

> Mere mortals forgive better on a full stomach, so how about dinner on Saturday? I'll call for you at eight-thirty if you promise to leave the briefcase at home.

And this time it was signed. 'Luke'. As if she hadn't guessed. But she realised with irritation that it wasn't followed by either a phone number or an address. Mr Luke Hunter was apparently too arrogant to consider that her answer might not be an automatic 'yes'.

What was more, it still wasn't clear who he thought was doing the forgiving. And, although Folly stared at the slip of pasteboard with the kind of intensity that fortune-tellers reserved for Tarot cards, she didn't know exactly what he had in mind. . . Or what she planned to do about it when she found out.

But at least the mystery was nearing a solution—even if she had no idea why Luke Hunter should want to go out to dinner with a woman whose sole contact with him up till now had been violently centred somewhere round the solar plexus.

Folly smiled at the memory. She had to give him full marks for originality. And romance—although ideally, if she had been advising him as a florist, she would have suggested roses instead of the more exotic lilies and orchids he had chosen. Roses always seemed more personal; the very epitome of romance. As well as being her own personal favourite. . .

But his choice of blooms was hardly the issue. The question was, did she want to go out to dinner with him? No, it wasn't. Folly shook her head. The question was, why was she even considering it? The last thing she needed right now was a relationship with a man like Luke Hunter. . .

Except that she hadn't dreamt about Tony for the past three nights, so perhaps he was doing some good. On a sort of homoeopathic basis, perhaps—as a counter-irritant? And who on earth was talking about relationships, anyway? All the card said was 'dinner'. And 'dinner' sounded an awful lot more enticing than the prospect of another hamburger from the greasy little café down the road.

And Luke was local—he might be able to help her with her flat-hunting. Folly felt almost embarrassed at herself for the ease with which she was finding these excuses—and for the fact that she seemed to have slipped into mental first-name terms with this man who was, after all, a stranger.

Perhaps she should get his number from directory enquiries. Her hand hovered over the phone, then pulled away. In the end she decided to leave it to fate. If Luke Hunter was prepared to take a chance then so was she. What was she risking, after all? He was unlikely to have her arrested again, and an unwanted pass might seem like fair payment for a few hours spent out of the confines of her depressing little room.

She could cope with anything Luke Hunter threw at her. Couldn't she?

He probably wouldn't even come. It was eight o'clock, and Folly was cursing the cowardice, or whatever it was, that had prevented her from discovering Luke's number and ringing to refuse the invitation. She was also cursing the stupidity that had made her accept—even by default—a dinner date with a man so obviously well-heeled without considering the depleted state of her wardrobe. And without even checking where it was he planned to take her.

She didn't even know if it was casual or formal, for goodness' sake! Not that she had many choices. If it was even slightly formal she had only one. Shivering a little in the silky bra and pants set that was all she was wearing, Folly held her only 'good' dress up against her to judge the effect.

It suited her as well as it always did, the creamy-white silk throwing her olive skin into greater contrast against her thick raven hair and dark Mediterranean eyes. But she wasn't entirely satisfied. The dress had been a gift from her mother, and, although it was pretty enough, it had never been one of her favourites.

The draping cut and narrow pleats of the dress harked back to the costumes of ancient Greece, emphasising her un-English appearance—and her youth. She looked almost demure, she thought disparagingly, glaring at her reflection as if her dilemma were all the mirror's fault. Was that how Luke Hunter saw her? A little foreign girl, to be swept off her feet by his English wealth and power?

But, whatever her doubts, she had to admit that the dress did look good, and it wasn't too formal if her escort turned up in jeans. He hadn't looked the scruffy type, but she had no way of telling what his idea of dinner might be. All her misgivings came flooding back. What was she doing, anyway, going out with a man she didn't know the first thing about? If he even turned up. . .

But somehow the thought that he might not made her feel even crosser.

'Why don't you ever stop to think, Aphrosyne Taylor-Agathangelou?' She had heard the complaint so often from mother, teachers and friends that she could hear their concerted voices in her head. 'There goes Folly,' her mother would have said. 'My little Aries ram, rushing in where angels fear to tread.' And it was true. She knew it was true. But somehow she never saw it until *afterwards*. . .

There was a rap on the door, and the maid's reedy voice.

'Miss Taylor?'

'Come in!' she called, still engrossed in her reflection. 'What is it—what do you want?'

But this time the voice that answered her was deep and rich—and she had heard it before. 'I'm not sure I ought to tell you. At least, not in front of the maid.'

'Luke!' Folly spun round, clutching the dress against her in panic. He was standing in the doorway, his lean frame clad in a loose-fitting tawny-coloured suit that seemed to emphasise the taut muscle that lay beneath it. Behind him, the maid was hovering.

'You're early!' she threw at him accusingly. As if that were the problem, rather than the fact that she was half-naked. 'Do you mind?'

'Not at all.' He was looking at her with frank enjoyment that seemed untainted by any sort of guilt. 'Do I gather you do? You shouldn't—you look delicious.' And, while Folly tried to gather her wits for a retort, he turned to the maid. 'Thank you, Elise.' He pressed something into her hand, and, from the faint rustle and the look of satisfaction on the girl's face, Folly guessed resentfully that it wasn't a coin. 'Off you go, now.'

Belatedly Folly realised that she should stop her. 'Wait! Take Mr Hunter back down to Reception——' But the tip seemed to have produced as effective a deafness as if it had been crammed in the girl's ears, and the door slammed shut behind her.

'Mr Hunter, you're early,' she said again, in her best 'No-nonsense' voice. 'As you can see, I'm not quite ready. If you could wait downstairs. . .'

But the deafness must have been catching. 'I know how women hate trying to dress when they don't know where they're going,' he said, as though that explained it all. 'So I thought I would come round a little early, in case you needed advice. That dress is great, by the way. Just right. Though it seems a shame to cover up what's underneath. . .'

'Mr Hunter, that is none of your business.' Behind the all-too-flimsy barrier of the dress, Folly could feel a deep red blush spreading to parts of her body she hadn't known *could* blush. She felt neon-pink, pulsating. 'And I don't need your advice. Now would you please get out of my bedroom while I finish dressing? Or I'll ——'

'You'll what? Hit me again? What a violent woman you are, Miss Aphrosyne Taylor-Agathangelou. Do you always threaten your dates?'

Her visitor wandered nonchalantly over to the window and looped back the curtain to peer out. 'Don't mind me,' he said in tones of such infuriating kindliness that Folly began to think that perhaps violence might be a good idea. 'I won't look. Scout's honour.'

She hesitated for a moment, her eye on the bathroom door. But to reach it she would need to walk within feet of her visitor—and release her grip on the dress with one hand to open the door. And the glint in his eye as he had enjoyed her earlier discomfiture convinced her he would not miss such an opportunity to embarrass her further.

While his back was turned, then... As swiftly as she could she dropped the dress over her head and wriggled into it—only to emerge from its temporary darkness to see Luke Hunter's eyes upon her, and a look of mocking appreciation on his face.

'You looked!'

But her guest was cheerfully unrepentant. 'I forgot—I was never a Scout.' Somehow he made it sound like a valid excuse. 'I always had better things to do than play with woggles. And, after seeing the back of that very fetching little wisp you were wearing, I thought it would be a shame to miss the front. Particularly since you were wearing it in my honour.'

'In your honour!' This time the red that flooded Folly's face was of annoyance—until the thought occurred to her that there had been several other sets of serviceable underwear she could have chosen. She hadn't worn these since her last date with Tony... So why...? 'Oh, don't be ridiculous, Mr Hunter,' she snapped back. 'I can assure you that my taste in underwear is nothing to do with you. Now, if you'll excuse me, I just want to tidy my hair.'

With as much dignity as she could muster, she stalked past him into the bathroom. But from the soft laugh that followed her she had the ominous feeling that he was no more convinced by her protests than she was herself.

* * *

'So how come a nice girl like you is trailing the streets of London beating up strangers under an assumed name?'

Folly didn't answer immediately. But this time the pink tinge to her face and the open-mouthed gasping which delayed her were not due to her dining companion's impudence.

'I did warn you the soup was hot.' Luke grinned. 'You do rush into things, don't you? Thai food is to be approached with caution if you're not used to it. No—don't drink; that makes it worse. Here; have some rice.'

The blandness of the rice he forked helpfully into her still-open mouth did help to quench the fires. 'Very funny, Mr Hunter.' But it was difficult to sustain indignation when every other thing the man said was calculated to infuriate. 'I told you; Folly is just a nickname. Aphrosyne is my real name, but people over here find it rather a mouthful—like the Greek part of my surname. There's only a certain number of times a person can take spelling "Aphrosyne Agathangelou" over the phone.'

'I can see that. But why Folly? Was it derived from your character?' His tone was innocent, just asking for information.

'I'm afraid not.' She took another, more cautious sip of the soup. 'It's a translation—Aphrosyne is the Greek for foolishness; for folly. Nothing to do with rushing in where angels fear to tread.' Although even as she said it the thought rushed through her mind that that was exactly what she was doing now. Somehow Luke Hunter in the flesh seemed a whole lot less easy to 'cope with' than she had envisaged.

He was still looking at her; appraisingly, with a sort of lazy sensuality that made something inside her twist tight. 'And you prefer your alias? I'm not sure I do. With that colouring, Aphrosyne suits you better. It's a pretty name. And unusual. I take it you're part Greek?'

She nodded. 'On my father's side. My mother is English. She went to Greece on holiday and never came back. I was born a rather scant seven months after the wedding. On April Fool's Day, to be exact——' She stopped in mid-sentence. Now what on earth had possessed her to tell Luke either of those facts? She got quite enough teasing about her name without letting on about her all-too-appropriate birth-date—and her parents' hasty marriage was hardly his concern.

But he didn't seem shocked, or embarrassed, or even taken aback. And he didn't tease her. 'So you were their folly. Very romantic. Or was it?'

It somehow didn't surprise her that he should go straight to the heart of things. 'Oh, yes. They've always been very happy together.' Her voice softened as she spoke.

Luke raised his glass and took a sip of wine. 'A holiday romance with a happy ending. . .Quite a fairy tale. Your mother was a lucky woman.'

'They were both lucky. Unfortunately it doesn't seem to run in the family.' It came out without her thinking, and Folly cursed herself for letting him slip so easily past her guard. What was it about this man? Since she'd met him things that were normally buried fathoms deep seemed to be floating to the surface. And she wasn't sure that she was ready for such exposure.

The questioning look in his eyes showed he hadn't missed the slip. 'Cinderella's coach didn't turn up the second time around?'

There was nothing to do but brazen it out. 'It was there on the horizon. But, on the stroke of midnight,

Prince Charming turned back into a rat.' She was surprised to find that she could joke about it.

He looked at her consideringly. 'I'd say you were almost over him. And some day we all have to find out the difference between romance and real life. Maybe you were lucky to get it over with so soon.'

The touch of cynicism struck a slightly sour note, but it lasted only a few seconds before the teasing tone was back. 'So now you're English Folly, not Greek Aphrosyne,' he mused. 'But you don't sound particularly Greek. Have you been in England long?'

She shook her head. 'Only six months. But I always spoke English with Mum, and I went to an English school in Athens. My grandmother paid for it—she never really came to terms with Mum's moving abroad, and I think that was her way of making sure I never lost the other half of my inheritance.'

'So what brought you over here now?' They had lapsed into everyday small talk, but a strand of their previous intimacy still infused Luke's questioning. As if he really needed to know. . .

Folly frowned, trying to remember how it had been. 'A combination of things,' she said at last. 'Gran died, and left her house to me, so someone had to arrange about selling it. And I was beginning to feel I wanted to strike out on my own. Then I read in a magazine about floristry courses at Chipchester College and decided that sounded like me.'

Luke looked puzzled. 'But why floristry? Surely, with your background, something in the hotel line would have made more sense?'

She shook her head, flattered by his interest in what, to a man like Luke Hunter, must be very small beer. 'My parents' hotel is very small; they didn't really need me to help run it. And I wouldn't be happy working for anyone else. I wanted my own business—almost anything would have done.'

'And you enjoy floristry?'

Folly shrugged. 'In most ways, though I find it a bit frustrating at times. The actual work can be a bit fiddly—sometimes an arrangement just won't go right and I have to restrain myself from hurling it across the room. But I've got a good sense of design, and I like the contact with customers. In fact, I thought of interior designing, but you really need the right connections for that.'

She grinned. 'Lots of nice rich friends to give you commissions while you find your feet. Floristry comes cheaper, and I knew Gran's money would only stretch so far.'

'Very businesslike.' He sounded impressed, then spoilt it by lapsing back into the mocking tone of their earlier conversation. 'So you do sometimes think before you act? Which reminds me. . .' He leaned back in his chair with an air of smug satisfaction on his face. 'I don't think you've thanked me yet for not pressing charges the other day.'

'Thanked you!' The sheer effrontery of it made her gulp her fiery mouthful unthinkingly, and for a moment she was doubly speechless. 'If you hadn't been so awkward about it I doubt if that constable would even have taken my name and address. We were sorting it out quite nicely until you stuck your oar in. And you were doing it deliberately. You must have known that girl was nothing to do with me—you just wanted revenge.'

He might have had the grace to look a little sheepish, she thought. But no—lions didn't look sheepish. Not unless they were wolves in sheep's clothing. . .But her mental menagerie was beginning to get rather confused. And whatever clothes Luke Hunter wore, they were most definitely his own.

'Not revenge,' he said reprovingly. 'Though you did make rather a big dent in my dignity. But once I'd had a chance to calm down a little I realised that what I wanted was you. After you'd arrived in my life with such a bang I had no intention of letting you walk straight out again.'

'And you thought I'd be nice and accessible in gaol?' Her indignation was mingled now with pleasure. He had wanted to see her again. . .

'I didn't plan to let it go that far. I just wanted to teach you a lesson—and make sure I had your name and address. If I'd asked you for it you'd probably have punched me in the eye.'

It was impossible not to feel mollified by the explanation, although Folly did her best not to show it. 'I still think an apology would be in order.'

'That's very good of you. I accept unreservedly.' He signalled the waiter, who came bustling up to clear the table for the next course. 'And in return I will continue to patronise your establishment. And I promise not to embarrass you in front of the paying public by pointing out the mildew on your roses.'

'My roses don't have mildew. I'm very proud of them, in fact. They're my favourite flowers.'

Folly blushed a little at the thought that Luke might think she was hinting, but he didn't respond. She was taken aback to realise just how far her reservations about seeing him had disappeared. She felt a twinge of apprehension, but then the reminder that he was a customer of the Rose Bowl made her feel more comfortable.

Not that such a tenuous connection was any real guarantee of respectability, but it did make him seem less of a stranger. She could imagine herself mentioning it to her mother—'Oh, yes, Mum; that Luke Hunter man is one of the shop's best customers. In fact I had dinner with him the other night. . .'

After all, anyone might have dinner with a customer. It was good for business. Nothing foolish about it at all. . .

But then she realised that the customer in question was looking at her as if he could read her thoughts—and found them highly amusing. It suddenly seemed very important to divert his attention. 'What starsign are you, Luke?' she asked on impulse, remembering her mother's comment.

Unfortunately, she felt almost certain that he had guessed the reason for her sudden change of tack. A lazy grin spread over his face. 'Leo, I believe. Why—do you believe in all that kind of thing?'

Leo—the lion. It was almost frighteningly appropriate. 'Oh I don't know,' she said evasively. 'My mother's very interested in it, and I have to know a bit about it as a florist. People quite often want birthday arrangements with a zodiacal theme. Or they might want to know someone's birth-flowers.'

'Birth-flowers?' He sounded interested. 'I've heard of birthstones, but I didn't realise there was a horticultural equivalent. So what are yours?'

'Oh, nothing very glamorous, I'm afraid. I'm an Aries, which is honeysuckle and sweetpeas—because they're spring flowers, I suppose. But I also get "all thorny plants and bushes", which I suppose covers roses as well. As I said, they're my real favourites——'

She broke off, suddenly realising that her words might be taken the wrong way. 'Though I loved your orchids and lilies,' she added hastily. 'Do you always woo your ladies so extravagantly? Not that I'm complaining, of course.'

'As a florist? Or as one of "my ladies"?' It was her own phrase, but somehow the way he said it made it sound as if he kept a harem. 'But no, since you ask; no, I don't. Only the more special of my ladies get the orchid and lily treatment.' He paused. 'Like you, Folly. I knew you were special the moment I recovered consciousness and saw your face swimming before my eyes.'

Folly felt suddenly breathless, as if something had tightened beneath her rib-cage. Despite the teasing undertones, his voice had modulated into seriousness, and she wasn't sure how to react. 'It was probably just concussion,' she joked at last. 'Perhaps you should go to the doctor.'

'Perhaps. But I'm not sure I want to be cured of you, Aphrosyne Taylor-Agathangelou.' He took another sip of his wine and stretched back in his chair, watching her. 'I think I'd rather you lingered a while yet. So you liked the flowers? I'd forgotten I had a professional to impress.'

Beneath the table she felt his legs brush against hers, and the tenuous contact made her shiver. 'They were beautiful—I just wondered what made you choose those in particular. Instead of roses, for example. . .'

The temperature in the restaurant seemed to drop by several degrees, and the eyes that met hers across the table glittered threateningly gold. 'I've never been very fond of roses,' he said dismissively. 'I don't like the thorns.'

Folly shivered, without knowing why. His words were trivial—but they had an ominous sound. But, before she could work out why, his tone had changed again. And the eyes that challenged her across he table were just brown eyes, filled with lazy amusement.

'So tell me about this Rose Bowl of yours,' he said, leaning back and signalling the waiter for another bottle of wine. 'What made you choose that particular shop?' If he had meant to distract her Luke Hunter had chosen the right bait. It felt so good to have someone to talk to. Folly's enthusiasm took over and she found herself pouring out the whole story.

CHAPTER THREE

'So LET's get this straight.' As the waiter cleared away the debris of their meal, Luke Hunter was looking at Folly across the table with an expression in his eyes that she found hard to classify. 'You're telling me that when you arrived in England less than six months ago you'd never been here before?'

'Well, only occasionally, to stay with my grandmother.' What point was he was trying to make? 'But I really don't remember much about that.'

'Right. And you decided to take up floristry because you saw a course advertised in a magazine?'

She was beginning to feel hunted, but something told her that the only defence against a man like Luke was attack. 'I told you, I didn't much mind what I did. I just wanted a business where I could be independent——'

But he gave her no time to explain. 'How long was the course?'

'It would have been a year. But I——'

'But you had an unhappy love-affair and decided to cut it short; yes, I know. And now you've come down to London with no accommodation apart from that grotty little hotel, and signed a lease on a shop you've never seen before, with no independent survey, no up-to-date trading figures and no solicitor to check the terms of the agreement?'

By now Folly's hackles were definitely up. 'And what was I supposed to do?' she countered. 'Let the place go? It's absolutely perfect for what I want, and there was someone else after it. They were making up their minds the next day, so I couldn't risk——'

'How do you know?'

She broke off, puzzled. 'How do I know what?'

'That there was someone else after it?'

His voice was deceptively innocent, and she was led right into the trap. 'Well, because she told me, of course. Miss Philimore. . .' Her voice tailed off. 'Oh. I see. You mean she might have been lying?'

'It has been known to happen. She probably thought you needed gingering up.' He looked at her cynically. 'Little did she know that she had just landed one of the world's greatest exponents of "leap before you look" as a buyer, or she'd probably have persuaded you to buy London Bridge and a stake in a Peruvian goldmine at the same time.'

But Folly had spent twenty-three years being told that she rushed into things too fast, and she wasn't about to let it get to her now. 'Oh, don't exaggerate, Luke. Perhaps I was a bit hasty, but I did read the lease, you know. It seemed fair enough. And when you say "no up-to-date trading figures", it was only the last six months that hadn't been prepared. And she explained that. Her accountant——'

'Had been suddenly called away to the funeral of a close relative? Or was he stricken with glandular fever? Don't be more of an idiot than you can help, Folly. She's trying to sell the place; she'd make damn sure that those figures were available if she wanted them to be seen. Since they're not, it's a fair bet that they show something she doesn't want you to know. And I could even make an educated guess what that might be.'

His arrogant air of certainty was beginning to infuriate her. Folly took a deep breath. 'You? What do you know about floristry?' She would not lose her temper.

'Nothing.' His expression was almost grim. 'But I know enough about business to realise that when a rival opens up just down the road it's likely to have an adverse effect on my profits.'

What she had expected him to say, Folly wasn't quite sure. But whatever it was, it wasn't this. She looked at him in genuine puzzlement. 'A rival? What do you mean? I didn't see another florist's, Luke. And I'm not completely naïve. I walked all round the area to check out the competition, and the nearest was streets away. That should be plenty in London terms.'

'In London terms? What do you know about London? What do you know about England, for that matter? But in any case, you're wrong. You have a rival about a hundred yards from your door—and bang on Oxford Street, unlike the Rose Bowl. It's quite a recent development—within the last six months. And I wouldn't be in the least surprised to find that that's why your Miss Philimore has decided to get out.'

Folly stared back at him, trying to control her mounting panic. Had she really missed something that obvious? Frantically she retraced her steps in her mind. Yes; she had definitely walked down towards Oxford Street; of course she had. There had been restaurants and clothes-shops—but no florists. He was just trying to frighten her. 'I don't believe you, Luke,' she said with more confidence than she felt. 'If there had been anything there I'd have seen it.'

'It was probably too big for you to see.'

The cryptic remark made her explode with frustration. 'What the hell's that supposed to mean?'

'It means, what about the department store on the corner?'

'That place?' Folly was taken aback. Of course she had seen the massive building on the junction with

Oxford Street. She had even vaguely registered that it sold flowers, but it had never occurred to her to regard it as a serious rival.

Her heart-rate started to calm down. 'Oh, they must have been selling flowers for ages, Luke. If it was going to harm our sales it would have done it by now. And anyway, a department store couldn't really compete with a specialist shop like the Rose Bowl. They just couldn't give the same level of service.'

His face didn't lighten. 'This isn't just any department store. This is a big Oxford Street site we're talking about, Folly. And although you're right that they've been selling flowers for a long time, they underwent a massive re-fit recently. I shop there a lot as it's so handy for my offices, and I seem to recall that about six months ago the floristry section was moved from an upper floor where no one ever saw it right on to the Oxford Street frontage.'

'But even so. . .'

But his voice went relentlessly on. 'They've even given it a full display window, Folly. I'm convinced that could be what's affected the Rose Bowl's profits recently. You should check it out. You might be in for a shock.'

But Folly's moment of panic had subsided, and she felt her natural confidence reassert itself. After all, in this field it was she and not Luke Hunter who was the expert. 'All right, then; I'll go and have a look at it tomorrow,' she said cheerfully. 'And it's good of you to be concerned. But the fact that I've never been to England before doesn't make me a complete bumpkin. Athens is a capital city too, you know. Honestly, you Londoners are so insular! It's not the only place in the world.'

'No—no, it's not.' He was speaking slowly and

carefully, as if he wondered after all whether her English was up to scratch. 'I'm sure many people live happy and contented lives without ever sighting Piccadilly Circus,' he went on. 'But, on the other hand, probably very few of them decide on a whim to spend their entire capital on a shop in a strange city in a country they know nothing about, without doing the most elementary homework. I'm beginning to think your name is more apt than I realised. You know what they say about fools and their money. . .'

But that was too much for Folly. She could feel the anger bubbling up inside her, made all the worse by knowing, in one corner of her mind, that he was right. 'Yes,' she retorted. 'And I know what they say about people who invite other people out to dinner and then spend the whole time trying to depress them and ruin their lives.'

She didn't, actually, but if there wasn't a proverb to fit then it was time someone wrote one. 'Of all the patronising——Oh! What's the point of telling me what I should have done? I've done it now, and I'm damn well going to make a success of it, Mr Hunter. So if you can't be more positive——' she folded her napkin and threw it down like a gauntlet on the table between them '——then I don't see why I should stay here and listen to you.' And, glaring furiously into those mocking brown-gold eyes, she pushed back the chair as if to go.

But his laugh arrested her. Somehow it wasn't as if he was laughing *at* her, but rather with her—against the world. 'Well, you've got determination; I'll say that for you.' He sounded almost admiring, but then went and spoilt it all by adding, 'Although I suppose if you've gone through life getting yourself into situations like this you would be bound to develop a fairly strong streak of subbornness by now.'

'Goodbye, Luke.' She bent to pick up her handbag.

But he shook his head. 'Don't go, Folly. I'm sorry if I pitched it strong, but you'll never get anywhere in business by sticking your head in the sand. And until we've looked honestly at the mess you've landed in, we can't hope to work out the best way out of it.'

Slowly she subsided back into her seat. 'What do you mean, "we"? This is nothing to do with you, Luke. I'll manage. I can——'

'You can stop being so touchy and have the sense to take advice when it's offered you.' His voice softened. 'I do know what I'm talking about, Folly. I've lived in London all my life, and I've built up three businesses from scratch.'

'Three?' It seemed a little excessive, even for someone as larger-than-life as Luke Hunter. 'What happened to the other two?'

His eyes danced with amusement. 'They went bust,' he said. 'But all that means is that I know damn well what *not* to do. And my present venture is going strong.' At that moment the bill arrived, and when Luke handed his card to the waiter, Folly noticed again its platinum colour. . .

'So I see,' she said drily. 'But presumably you know something about what you do, whereas floristry——'

'Floristry is a business, like any other,' Luke said firmly. 'And like most businesses, it's basically about selling. Which is something I do know about. My company provides a sales and marketing function for all kinds of firms who prefer to concentrate on what they're good at and leave the selling of it to us. So you see, though I wouldn't dream of advising you how to arrange a bouquet, there are plenty of other areas where my experience could be of help.'

But then he would believe that. Folly knew that she should get up and leave. Something told her that once she let this irrepressible man weave his way into the fabric of her life it would be almost impossible to get rid of him. She could manage alone... The Rose Bowl was her enterprise; her baby. The last thing she wanted was to have some overbearing man muscling in.

And yet something kept her sitting there; kept her listening. 'Good girl.' Luke had taken her silence for assent. 'Now, let's look on the dark side for a moment.' He said it almost with relish, as if dark sides were what he liked best. 'The way I see it, you have three main problems. Number one; you have nowhere to live. Number two; the only thing you know about London is how to spell it. And number three; you've signed your way into a deal you know nothing about and which has almost certainly sold you up the river. Does that sum it up?'

'I suppose so.' Why did he have to make her feel so stupid? 'Pretty hopeless, isn't it? But it's not your problem, Luke. So if you'll excuse me——'

'Sit down.' This time it was a command, and she found herself obeying unthinkingly. 'No problem is hopeless if you've got the courage to look it in the face. And, as it happens, the first two of yours are quite easy to solve. The third one may take a bit more work, but then that's half the fun.' He smiled that predatory smile she remembered so well from their first meeting. 'Say thank you to Uncle Luke.'

'Thank you, Uncle Luke.' The words were invested with as much sarcasm as she could muster. 'Am I allowed to ask what these brilliant solutions are?'

'But naturally. Your first problem as I recall from

my masterly analysis, is that you have nowhere to live except a hotel that's rapidly running out of vases. I, on the other hand, have a flat——'

'Oh, no. No way.' Folly's mouth set in a grim line. If he thought she was falling for that. . .

'If you'd just let me finish before diving in to protect your honour you might find it wasn't actually endangered,' Luke retorted with dangerous mildness. 'What I was saying was that I have a flat which is not currently in use. It's a company flat; I keep it for entertaining mostly. And it's only a few blocks away from your shop. I could let you have it for a few months until you get sorted out.'

'Oh.' He had rather taken the wind out of her sails. 'Well, thank you. But what about rent? I doubt if I could afford anything that central.'

'I don't remember mentioning rent; and I certainly don't intend to charge it. No——' He held up his hand as she opened her mouth to protest. 'No, don't argue. Quite apart from any other reason, if I charged you rent, it would give you security of tenure. This is just a temporary arrangement, with you as my guest. Yes or no, Folly?'

'Yes, then.' He did have a habit of railroading her into things, but she knew she would be crazy to refuse. 'But what was the other solution?'

'Oh, that's quite straightforward. I know this city like the back of my hand, and I love every yard of it. We've got the rest of the weekend ahead of us. So how about me introducing you to your new home?'

She had been planning to spend her Sunday flat-hunting, but, with a surge of gratitude, she realised that that would no longer be necessary. 'Thanks, Luke. I'd like that.' She felt her mouth twist into a wry smile. 'So that's two problems down. But even you don't know what to do about the third, do you? And that's the big one.'

'I don't know how to solve it,' he corrected. 'But I know what to do about it. And that's to make sure of our facts. Until we do that, we don't even know if there really is a problem. So if you let me take a copy, I'll give that lease you signed to my company solicitor and get him to go through it with a magnifying glass. And I'll get my accountant to chase your vendor's elusive accountant and get some figures for the last few months. Then we'll work out our strategy. And then we'll take them by storm. Right?'

'Right.' She paused. 'Take who by storm?'

'No nit-picking,' he said severely. 'Anyone who needs it. I'm still working on the broad business vision here, not pettifogging little details. Now let's get you back to that hotel and pick up your luggage.'

'What, tonight?' Folly was momentarily assailed by the enormity of what she was doing. She had come to London to take control of her own life, and now she was meekly handing over the reins to this man who was almost a stranger. And how on earth would she explain it to her mother?

But she knew she wouldn't refuse. Luke Hunter might be technically a stranger. But something told her that she could trust him more than any of her so-called friends.

Next morning, Folly woke up half expecting that it would all turn out to be a dream. But the light that filtered through the curtains as she sat up in bed soon convinced her that, unlikely though it seemed, she really had left the discomforts of her hotel behind her for good.

But as for what she had exchanged it for—that still

seemed more like fantasy than waking reality. Luke's company flat might be small—although, compared with some of the broom-cupboards she had inspected, it ranked as positively palatial—but it was luxurious in style. No doubt the clients he entertained here were people who expected the best.

But even so, a four-poster bed and, if her memory wasn't playing tricks on her, a sunken marble bath with golden taps. . . And the carpeting throughout so soft and thick that it was like walking on sheepskins. . .

No doubt it was all in keeping with Luke's Leo magnificence—a fitting lair for the King of Beasts. But Folly found it all rather overwhelming, as if she had suddenly been spirited away by a magic carpet and found herself in some Sultan's harem. Which, at one point last night, she remembered with a rising tide of embarrassment, was just about what she had decided was happening. . .

At first, when he had suggested that they ought to celebrate her 'housewarming' with champagne, she had thought he was joking. But then she had heard that soft, unmistakable 'pop' from the tiny kitchen and her host had re-entered carrying a chilled bottle which the trace of vapour trailing from its neck proclaimed to be the real thing.

That was when she had made a fool of herself. Again. It had suddenly borne in upon her that it was almost midnight and that she was in a strange flat in a strange city, with a strange man who was plying her with champagne. And so, in true Arien fashion, she had decided to take the bull by the horns.

Standing with her feet firmly planted in the centre of that luxurious carpet, she had made her position absolutely clear. 'Look, Luke, I don't know where you think this evening is leading,' she had plunged in determinedly. 'But one place it certainly isn't going is through that door.' She had gestured towards the bedroom that he had shown her shortly before. 'And you needn't think that a couple of glasses of champagne will make any difference. In fact, I think you'd better go. I'm determined——'

'To sell your honour dearly; yes, I know.' Luke's lazy voice had mocked her. 'But unfortunately, at the moment, I'm not even in the bidding. I'm afraid your rather fervid imagination is running away with you. Just now, all I want is a glass of this rather splendid champagne.'

His voice had hardened almost imperceptibly, as if the lion's soft paw had unsheathed the tips of its claws. 'My champagne, in my flat. And I intend to have it. So I'm afraid you'll just have to contain your Aries impatience a little longer—unless, of course, you intend to call the porter and have me put out. . .'

Then he had deposited the champagne bottle on a small occasional table, next to a sleek ivory-coloured object that Folly had just about recognised as a phone, and she had watched in horrified fascination as he'd picked up the receiver and started to tap out a number.

'Hello, Bert? Hunter here. A friend of mine will be borrowing the flat for a while—a Miss Taylor. And I think she has something to say to you. . .'

He had even held the receiver out in Folly's direction, but she'd blushed crimson with embarrassment and pushed it away. By now it must have been obvious to her host that she had put him down as a direct descendant of Casanova, Don Juan or Jack the Ripper—or possibly a combination of all three. But to her surprise, he hadn't seemed angry at all. In fact, he had almost seemed to understand.

Folly slipped out of bed and wriggled her toes in the

thick, silky pile of the carpet. Remembering. Luke hadn't said anything to increase her embarrasment. In a mild voice he had just asked the porter to come up, with some story about a tap dripping in the kitchen. Then he had steered her to a chair, rather than the sofa, which would probably have provoked a new attack of 'imagination'. And when the man had arrived, Luke had offered *him* a glass of champagne and then shown him through to the kitchen and shut the door.

The fact that he had never asked the man if he'd been able to fix the problem, Folly suddenly realised, was proof enough that the supposedly leaky tap was just an excuse to provide her with a chaperon. She supposed she ought to be pleased at this fresh evidence of Luke's sensitivity. She *was* pleased. . . The porter had stayed almost half an hour—presumably dismantling and re-constructing a perfectly healthy tap—and by the time he had left, it was true, she'd felt far more relaxed.

It was just that somehow she'd also felt disappointed. . . As if Luke had taken the demure image of the white dress, and missed the reality of the woman beneath it. As if he was treating her like a child. . .

But of course that was nonsense. The last thing she had wanted was for Luke to make a pass at her. Tony, she knew, would have seen an evening with her under those circumstances as a perfect battleground for another assault on her decision not to sleep with him. So it had been quite refreshing when Luke had said goodbye with no more than the lightest brush of his lips against her cheek.

Refreshing. . .but tantalising, too. Because by that time the single glass of champagne she had drunk had subtly eroded her defences. And she could still feel the moment when hope, as his face had bent towards her, had melted into an emotion much more like disappointment. And she had had to admit that she had wanted Luke Hunter to kiss her.

Properly...

Just then a knock at the door broke into her thoughts. Folly threw on a dressing-gown and hurried through to answer it, praying that it wouldn't be Luke. But, to her relief, the voice that greeted her from the other side of the oak door, though indistinct, was that of the porter she had met so briefly the evening before.

'Hello, miss? Bert Harris here. You decent?' His cheerful London accent seemed to bring her back down to earth, and she hurried to unlock the bolts and let him into the hallway.

To her surprise, the little man was almost hidden behind a large cardboard box. 'I've got you some bread and milk and stuff,' his muffled voice explained. 'Mr 'Unter don't keep the flat stocked, you see, 'cause it ain't used all that regular. So he asked me to bring some stuff up.'

'That's very kind of you.' Folly looked around for her handbag. 'How much do I owe you?'

'Me? Oh, nothing love. It's all gone on 'is account, so you don't need to worry. I'll just drop it off in the kitchen for you, shall I?'

Rather bemused, Folly stood back to let him past. She would have to repay Luke, of course, but it had been a very kind thought. Now she would be able to make a pot of tea and wake herself up properly. Her opinion of her benefactor leapt up another few notches as she followed his messenger through to the tiny kitchen, where the porter dumped his box on the only available surface and bent to open the fridge.

But Folly forestalled him. Luke Hunter might find it quite natural to have people fussing over him—presumably, with his wealth, it was something he'd have to get used to. But if felt strange to her independent nature. 'Just leave it there, Mr Harris,' she said awkwardly. 'I'll do the unpacking.'

'Well that's very good of you, miss. I am a bit pushed.' He made his way back to the hallway, dusting his hands off against his trousers. 'It's nice to see a young lady what knows her way around a kitchen for a change. You a relative of his?'

The apparent change of subject took Folly by surprise. 'What? Oh, no—we're not related.' And then she realised what the porter was *really* asking her. 'Mr Hunter is just a business acquaintance,' she added primly. 'But he's kindly offered to lend me the flat for a while, until I can find something more permanent.'

'Oh, right—I get you.' His tone was suddenly confiding. 'I knew you wasn't one of his usual harem— none of that lot look as if they could boil a kettle, never mind an egg. That's why I thought you must be his niece or something.' He laughed, so that it was impossible to take offence. 'Well, it's been nice meeting you, miss. If there's anything you want, just ring down and ask.'

'Thank you. I will.' But as she saw the man out Folly felt her mood unaccountably dampened. She suddenly remembered that she hadn't thought to offer him a tip—although, unlike the awful Elise, he hadn't seemed to expect any payment. But that wasn't the main thing that was bothering her. . .

Slowly she wandered back into the kitchen and started to unpack the boxful of food. Luke's generosity, she soon realised, had extended far beyond the porter's basic definition of 'bread and stuff'. There were enough provisions here to feed her for a week—and in far more luxury than she would have dreamt of buying for herself. But her pleasure in the gesture had been spoilt.

What had Bert Harris meant by 'one of his usual harem'? The question came sneaking into her mind and, once there, it proved difficult to dislodge. Not that Luke Hunter's sex-life was any of her business. She had only had dinner with him once, which hardly constituted an exclusive relationship.

But, on the other hand, he had told her that this was a company flat. Used for business entertaining, he had said. Whereas, according to the porter, it was something much more like a love-nest...

Folly felt an urge to wash, as if the words had been printed in dark, inky type in the headline of a tabloid newspaper and her hands might have picked up the stain. In her imagination, the little flat was suddenly peopled with the ghosts of tall, glamorous London women, with names like Wanda and Melissa, who knew when to tip porters and chambermaids and wouldn't have dreamt of unpacking their own shopping. They prowled across the soft carpet in their elegant high-heeled shoes, and then kicked them off to lounge seductively on the four-poster bed.

One of Luke Hunter's 'usual harem' wouldn't have wanted a porter to chaperon her. There would have been no danger of a Wanda's being mistaken for his niece. And he wouldn't have dismissed a Melissa with a kiss as light as thistledown—the sort of kiss he might had bestowed on a child.

She could imagine the kisses he would have shared with a woman like that... Folly closed her eyes and felt a fiery ball of mixed desire and jealousy settle in her stomach. He would have joined Melissa on the great bed, pressing her down against the coverlet and ravishing her long white neck with passionate kisses. And then, his mouth on hers——

'Oh, Luke,' she groaned, her eyes still closed and the tormenting vision still vivid on her mind. 'Why didn't you kiss me properly?' And instinctively she reached out her arms as if to circle his neck and draw him down into an imaginary embrace.

Only the solidity of the flesh she touched was very far from being imaginary. And the strong hands that slid round her waist were more real than any of her dreams.

CHAPTER FOUR

BY THE time Folly opened her eyes, Luke's lips were on hers, and all she could see was a few inches of gold-shadowed cheek and an ear. But vision no longer seemed important, compared to the tantalising, tormenting sensations with which the touch of his mouth was filling her. The warm, tangy scent of his skin went straight to her head, more quickly even than the champagne they had drunk together the evening before.

Crushed against him, Folly could no more have resisted than she could have held back the tides. He was a force of nature, elemental and raw. A desire that Tony had never evoked in her floated through her veins like liquid fire, and she found herself responding eagerly, wantonly, to his caresses. And yet, all the time, a part of her mind was holding back, afraid. Afraid of losing control; of losing herself in Luke's power.

But her body had no such fears. She could feel the hard strength of him pressing against her; his heat scorching her through the thin cotton of her nightdress as if he, too, were on fire. Her lips parted avidly to the questing thrust of his tongue. She seemed to be following instincts that had welled up from some deep, secret place that nothing—and no one—before had ever touched.

When at last Luke released her, she found herself clinging to the kitchen cabinet like a shipwrecked mariner to a rock. 'What——?' But her voice seemed to have been swept overboard somewhere in mid-voyage, and all that emerged was a croak.

'Now that's what I call a welcome.' The smug self-satisfaction in his tone jolted her back to something resembling consciousness. What had she been thinking of? Her face burned as she realised that while she had been soaring naïvely in previously unthought-of heights of bliss Luke Hunter had just been mentally carving another notch on his bed-post. No wonder he needed a four-poster. . .

'What the hell are you doing here, Luke? I didn't hear you come in.' She tried ineffectually to push him away, desperately trying to remember whether or not she had spoken those fateful words aloud. If he realised the effect he had had on her—was still having on her . . . The imprints of his hands still seemed to burn on her skin, as if at any moment her nightdress might burst into flames.

He was looking at her with amusement, and a sort of hungry satisfaction. 'Not quite the little innocent I thought you were, are you, my little Folly? That dress you were wearing last night was quite a disguise.'

'It was a present from my mother.' Her lips seemed to speak the words automatically, while her mind raced ahead.

'I see.' He sounded as if he did. 'Well, it was pretty enough. For a dutiful daughter. But for the woman. . .' He stood back to look down the line of her figure under the flimsy nightgown, his eyes caressing her as blatantly as if she had been naked. 'I'd like to see you in red, Folly. Have you got a red dress? If not you'll have to let me buy you one.'

He bent to kiss her again, but she thrust him away. 'Will you let me go?' That was better—she sounded angry now. A much more reasonable emotion. 'I buy my own clothes, Luke—and decide on the colour.' Except that red was her favourite colour, she thought confusedly. And now if she wore it Luke would be bound to think——

It was all getting far too complicated. So, like a true child of Aries, she dived back into the attack. 'And that's another thing, Luke Hunter. When you invited me to stay here, I didn't realise you planned to collect the rent in kind. If you're going to sneak round the place whenever it suits you, I'd rather be back in the hotel. At least the manager didn't pounce on me just because I shut my eyes for a few moments.'

Luke raised an eyebrow. 'Perhaps you didn't ask him to,' he mocked. 'Unless you're claiming that wasn't a "proper kiss"? Because, if you are, we could always try again. . .'

Folly felt her heart sink rapidly to somewhere in the basement. So he had heard those monumentally stupid words. It didn't leave her with much room to manoeuvre. 'I'd just got out of bed—I was half asleep,' she tried, without much conviction. 'I was dreaming. . . I'm not responsible for my dreams. And if I'd known you were here I would never ——'

'Then it's just as well I was here. It may have saved a lot of time.' Luke grinned, throwing into contrast the tiny creases round his mouth, and at the corners of his eyes. Folly felt a fresh wave of desire sweep through her, and was terribly afraid that he would see it too. In the gaze of those gleaming gold eyes she felt as transparent as glass.

'What do you mean?' It was a stupid question, but her mind was a blank of panic.

He raised his eyebrows. 'I mean that it might have taken me some time to see through your "innocent abroad" act. But now we've taken a short cut through the getting-to-know-you games. After that little performance you can hardly deny that you want me. Or you could, but I wouldn't believe you. So why don't we take it from there?'

He pulled her towards him again, but Folly slipped out of his arms and dodged away. 'No!' she squealed. Then, realising how witless that sounded, she fumbled on, 'I mean yes, I suppose I do find you attractive.' She made a stab at a brittle laugh, trying to fit herself to the image of one of his sophisticated London women—a Wanda or Melissa who would hardly be embarrassed by such an admission.

To judge by his continued expression of smug amusement, it hadn't been entirely successful. Folly took refuge in practicalities. 'But that doesn't mean I want things to go any further, Luke. It's my work that's important to me at the moment—I don't have time for casual affairs. And besides,' she added with a touch of spite, 'I don't think I'm really cut out to be a member of your harem.'

When he didn't react, she tried the laugh again. But he didn't laugh with her.

'What do you mean, my "harem"?' He sounded angry. 'What are you talking about, Folly? I don't pretend to be a monk, exactly, but I'm no Casanova, either. So why assume ——?'

'I wasn't assuming.' Why did men always try and make their failings out to be *her* fault? 'But if you were trying to keep it secret you should have made sure you bribed your porter not to talk.'

'Bert? What the hell has he been telling you?' Luke dropped his grip on her and turned to glance at the door, as if he intended to go and put his question to the man himself.

Folly realised belatedly that she might have stirred

up some trouble for her informant. 'Please don't blame him, Luke,' she improvised hurriedly. 'He mentioned in passing that you had a lot of female visitors, that's all. He seemed to think I was your niece.' She was surprised to realise just how much that thought still rankled. 'And anyway, I'm not criticising you; you have a perfect right to have as many women here as you want to.'

'I'm glad you think so.' He was hiding his anger better now, sounding more amused than annoyed. 'But I think you'll find ——'

But Folly didn't want to listen to his excuses. 'But on the other hand I have no intention of letting you add my name to the list, just because you've lent me this flat,' she lashed back. 'And if that means that you'd like your cosy little love-nest back, then that's fine. I'll move back to the hotel today.'

There; that was it. It was out now. She would have to move back into that horrible poky little hotel. But at least it would be better than letting herself be drawn in by his very potent brand of masculine attraction. Men like Luke Hunter didn't know the meaning of permanence—or fidelity. And after her experience with Tony she would never allow herself to be imposed on that way again.

She kept her eyes on his shirt-front, not daring to look at his face; to see his anger. Or not directly. But she could see it all the same, in the tremors that shook the broad plain of his chest as he struggled to contain his fury.

Silently she waited for the lion's roar. But when it came it wasn't quite as she had imagined. . .

'What a passionate little thing you are, Aphrosyne Taylor-Agathangelou——' A strange upheaval seemed to half strangle what he was saying. 'I think you'd better get dressed,' he managed at last. 'And then we'll have a little talk to Mr Harris. About my "harem". . .'

He didn't sound angry. And, as she steeled herself to look up into his face, Folly realised with shock that Luke Hunter was actually *laughing*.

'So you see, Bert, I think you gave this young lady the wrong idea about my visitors here. You forgot to mention that they are guests of the company, not mine personally. And that they stay here alone—or with their own partners. I rather suspect she has been imagining nameless orgies.'

'No. . .' Folly by this time was as red as the porter's uniform, and her voice almost inaudible. And she could feel the little man's shocked reproach when he replied. Or was it a little too obvious? Even through her own embarrassment she was cynically aware with one part of her mind that Bert Harris's interests would certainly not be served by going against a man as powerful as Luke. And that both of them would be well aware of it.

'Certinly not, miss.' He sounded sincere enough, and not a little worried. 'Strictly business purposes, like Mr 'Unter says. I never meant to imply no 'anky-panky.'

His self-righteous tone sparked off a flicker of rebellion. 'But you talked about his "harem", Bert. You said ——'

'I didn't say a word!' He looked apologetically across the desk at Luke. 'Only that's what we call 'em, the wife and me. Your young ladies what work for you, that is. We call 'em 'Unter's 'Arem. No disrespect intended, sir. Just a joke, like.'

He sounded so anxious that Folly was quite relieved to hear Luke put him at his ease. 'I know, Bert,' he said placidly. 'But I can see how it might have rung all the wrong bells with young Folly here. Perhaps in future you'd better save that sort of chat for people who know me. I'd hate to lose my reputation.'

He grinned, and the porter grinned back. But, before she could sort out just what her feelings were at this blatant example of male collusion, Folly found herself being steered towards the revolving doors to the street.

'Come on,' Luke urged her. 'I'll explain the programme in the car. But if we don't get moving now we'll mess up the schedule.'

'Get moving where? What schedule?' But if her companion had heard her he gave no sign.

At the side of the road, he raised an arm as if to hail a taxi, but it was the sleek black BMW they had travelled in the night before that came pulling towards them out of the traffic. Folly had to stifle the impression that he had conjured it by magic—or called it like a horse. Only when she saw the outline of a man's head in a peaked cap sitting in the driver's seat was the mystery explained.

'This is Sam, one of my company drivers,' explained Luke unnecessarily. 'He's going to drop us off and then pick us up later, after the tour.'

'Oh, I see.' In daylight Folly could really appreciate details of the luxury she had missed the previous evening. Like the polished wood that covered surfaces that would have been painted metal in any other car. . .'He's not driving us round, then?'

Luke shook his head. 'That way all you'd see would be tourists, shop windows and the back of an awful lot of taxis. I had in mind to give you an overview first of all. Then you can pick out what you'd like to see in more detail another time. How does that sound?'

'Fine. But Luke ——' Folly took a deep breath, and

prepared to resume the attack. But her host saved her the trouble.

'What Bert was saying about my "harem",' he said easily as the car purred forwards into the traffic. 'As you'd find out if you visited my company, I have quite a number of women working in my sales department. Hence the "harem" tag. And when the flat's not in use for entertaining clients I like to make it available to all my employees.'

He looked at her quizzically, as if trying to gauge her scepticism. 'Male *and* female,' he emphasised. 'They find it useful, especially those that live out of town. They can come in for a meal or a show and not have to worry about last trains, or driving back. But I can assure you that I don't exercise some kind of twentieth-century droit de seigneur over them for the privilege. Nor will I over you.'

His words carried the ring of truth, and Folly felt a flush of shame at what she had been imagining. After all he was doing for her, she had virtually accused him of trying to seduce her. But with part of her mind—the part that had stood back from their embrace—she was dimly aware that she had almost *wanted* to believe the worst. Because if Luke Hunter was really the man he seemed to be, she was in far greater danger. . .

'No, of course not. I'm sorry. . .' She had to force the words out, and she was aware they sounded painfully stiff. After all, it wasn't his fault that her feelings seemed to be running amok. 'Luke, it's very good of you to look after me like this. And to lend me the flat——'

'Don't thank me—thank my harem. It's them you're inconveniencing.' He dismissed her thanks with a wave of the hand. 'Don't worry about it, Folly. You're missing your tour. Look —here's St Paul's over on this side. And in a minute we'll be passing the Tower of London.'

'Oh!' Her embarrassment forgotten, Folly craned across him to see the dome which, until now, she had seen only in pictures. 'Can we stop, Luke?'

But he shook his head. 'I told you, overview first. And there's not far to go. The tour starts from Tower Bridge, and follows the river.'

A boat trip, then. That sounded fun. Folly realised that in her eagerness not to miss the sights she had ended up nestling right up against Luke Hunter's arm. But he didn't comment, and she felt reluctant to move. Besides, they were down by the river now, and she wanted to see the bridge. . .

'Oh, look, Luke! It's opening!' As the two sections of the bridge rose majestically into the air somehow it felt as if he had arranged it especially for her. She felt a thrill of excitement. 'Will our boat go right under it?'

'Our boat? Come on, this is the place.' The car drew to a halt by a green sward of carefully tended lawn which ran down from an impressive-looking office building towards the river.

'Yes—our boat for the tour. Will we go under the bridge?'

'Not unless you have even more an effect on me than I think you have. And I don't remember mentioning a boat. Come on; we're going in here.' And to Folly's surprise he started to lead her towards the building.

At the reception desk, he murmured a few words to the elaborately uniformed commissionaire and was shown respectfully towards the lift.

'All the way up.' The man stepped in and turned a key in a slot marked 'Security', then pressed a button. The door closed smoothly behind them, and the lift began to rise.

'Where are we going, Luke?' Folly was puzzled. Although it was an imposing building, it didn't seem special enough to be included on a tour. 'What is this place?'

'It's the head office of a company I do a fair amount of work for,' he explained as the floor numbers ticked silently across the display above the door. 'I promised you an overview, remember? And from the roof here I'll be able to show you right across London.'

'Oh. I see.' Folly didn't say anything, but she couldn't help thinking that the Post Office Tower would have been a better vantage-point, as well as being one of the 'sights' of London in its own right. But it was kind of him to have organised this—and at least they would command a good view of the bridge.

When they finally reached the top floor, the penthouse office was deserted. But Luke made his way through the panelled luxury as if he knew exactly where he was going.

'Through here,' he said at last, as he showed her out on to the roof.

At first she could see nothing except the river so many floors below them. The wind buffeted her ears as she wondered again what had made Luke bring her to this particular place. The view was good—but scarcely unique.

Then she realised he was still speaking to her. 'Here we are.' There was an odd note of pride in his voice, like a small boy showing off a new toy. 'Better than a boat, don't you think?'

She turned to look where he was pointing. Behind her, the flat expanse in the centre of the roof was dominated by something that perched there like a gigantic black dragonfly.

'Luke—you can't be serious!' As she watched, a

door swung open on the insect's side and an overalled figure jumped out and came hurrying towards them.

'Why not? I promised you an overview.' The air of smug satisfaction in Luke's voice was even more evident.

'But that—that's a *helicopter*.' Well done, Folly, she thought. Let's state the obvious, shall we? What was it about Luke Hunter that reduced her to such gibbering incoherence? She tried again. 'I mean, I thought you said we were going on a *boat* trip.'

'I don't think I did, you know. I said we were going to follow the river. We don't have any choice about that because this is only a single-engined job, so we're not allowed to fly over built-up areas. But the Thames route is pretty good anyway—we'll see a lot in a short time.'

While Folly was coming uncomfortably to terms with the fact that the reason they had to avoid built-up areas was to avoid too much carnage if they fell out of the sky, Luke turned to the man in the overalls, who was waiting respectfully for them to finish talking. That was another thing—it didn't help her to maintain her own sense of proportion when the rest of the world treated Luke Hunter as if he were some kind of royalty. . .

'All set?' He sounded quite excited and Folly found herself smiling at the way his dramatic gesture was bringing out the little boy in someone as sophisticated as Luke. At least it took her mind off the far less confident emotions that she was feeling on her own account.

'Yes, sir. The boss said you were to take her out for as long as you wanted, sir. Has the young lady been up before?'

Luke looked round at her enquiringly. 'Have you, Folly?'

She shook her head. 'No—and I'm not a hundred per cent sure that I want to start, Luke. Especially not right after breakfast. Do these things have sick-bags?' But she could feel her mouth smiling as she said it, belying her real nervousness. Deep down she knew that, however scared she was, she wasn't going to let Luke see it. And she felt a twinge of panic that, already, she cared so much for his opinion.

The other man ran quickly through a list of safety points. 'Although, of course, you won't need most of what I'm telling you,' he grinned. 'Not with Mr Hunter here as pilot. Just make sure you keep low, and remember that you always enter or leave a helicopter from a forward direction.'

Luke nodded in agreement. 'It's the tail rotors that do the damage—and I'd hate to spend my afternoon scraping you off the roof.' But Folly hardly heard him. She was still trying to take in the information she had just been given.

'*You're* going to fly this thing? But what about the pilot?' She looked pleadingly at the man in overalls as if he might step in and save her. Just why she found it so disturbing that Luke was planning to fly her she wasn't quite sure. But it seemed to underline just how completely she was falling into his power.

But her rescuer failed her. 'Oh, I'm just the mechanic, miss,' he grinned. 'But don't worry—my boss sets a lot of store by this little beauty. And Mr Hunter's never failed to bring it back yet.'

Which wasn't precisely what she was worried about, thought Folly as she ducked under the rotors and climbed up into the bubble-like cockpit. It wasn't Luke's competence that she was questioning. No doubt with typical Leo overkill, he would also turn out to be an expert in shooting rapids, taming wild horses, and leaping tall buildings with a single bound.

It was her own reactions that she was afraid of. And recently they seemed to be running out of control...

'So what do you think of it?' Luke had to raise his voice to make himself heard above the noise of the rotors, but the grin on his face made it clear that he, at least, was enjoying himself.

'It's wonderful,' Folly shouted back. And indeed it was. She had been taken by surprise by the suddenness with which the little helicopter had unstuck itself from the landing pad, and the unnerving rapidity of their ascent. But after the disorientation of the first few seconds she had found herself entranced by the city below her spread out like a living map.

The adrenalin was making her heart race with excitement. 'It's odd though,' she went on, still at the top of her voice. 'Not like a plane... At least in a plane it feels *logical* to be flying. Here, it doesn't, somehow, if you know what I mean.'

To her surprise Luke nodded. 'Yes, I do. It's the no visible means of support that gets to people.'

'That's exactly it!' She felt an absurd glow of pleasure that he had understood. 'I feel like a giant's yo-yo—as if there's someone up there just dangling me on a string. But it's a fabulous view.' She let her attention return to the vista that almost surrounded them, since the glass of the cockpit extended right under her feet. 'Oh, Luke! Is that the Tower of London?'

'Just next to the bridge? That's right. I always think you get a much better perspective on it as a real castle from up here.'

Looking down on the great White Tower and surrounding ramparts, Folly had to agree. It wasn't just a tourist showpiece. 'It's much bigger than I expected,' she admitted. 'And. . .menacing, somehow. Like a threat.' She shivered involuntarily.

But Luke seemed pleased. 'That's exactly why it was built; as a show of strength. William the Conqueror meant it to impress the rebellious Londoners with his power, as well as protecting them.'

He took one hand off the controls to sweep it out in a large gesture that took in the whole of the City of London. 'And imagine what it must have been like before all those modern office "towers" were built to dwarf it—especially if you happened to be a traitor. Can you see Traitor's Gate down there by the side of the river? And that's Tower Hill, where the public executions were held.'

'Like Anne Boleyn? I've always felt so sorry for her.' Folly felt quite proud of herself for remembering this snippet of English history. 'I can hardly believe I'm actually seeing the places where it happened.'

But Luke shook his head. 'No—Anne would have lost her head in decent privacy within the walls on Tower Green. Kings' wives were more privileged— even when they were accused of witchcraft. But I wouldn't waste your pity on her if I were you. She didn't deserve it.'

'What do you mean?' The callousness of Luke's words seemed out of character—and out of place for a mere historical discussion. 'Why shouldn't I be sorry for her?' She racked her brains to remember the rest of the story. 'She can't really have been a witch. Surely Henry VIII just wanted to get rid of her, didn't he, so he could marry someone else?'

'Quite the little historian.' There was a grim edge to his mocking that drew her attention, and Folly wished that she could see his face more clearly. But his gaze was rigidly fixed ahead as he steered the little helicopter up the meandering Thames. 'What else did they teach you in that Greek school of yours? Presumably not the minor detail that young Anne was a designing little minx who married Henry in cold blood to further her own ambitions—and then didn't even have the sense or decency to stand by her bargain.'

The unfairness of what he was saying took Folly's breath away. 'That's ridiculous, Luke. The fact that Henry was king doesn't mean she wasn't in love with him ——'

'Love?' Luke made the word sound like an oath, and Folly had the curious feeling that they were having two conversations at once—and only one of them was about ancient history. 'If she'd been in love with Henry she'd have agreed to be his mistress—not made him wait seven years for a divorce before she let him take her to bed. Seven years! You can hardly claim she was consumed by passion. Oh, no—she knew how to play her cards right. No sex without marriage—and a crown.'

The raw bitterness in his tone made Folly look round at him, startled. But his face, in icy profile, gave nothing away. A dreadful thought struck her.

'Luke—you're not married, are you?'

She was almost afraid to hear the answer, but, to her relief, he only laughed, though grimly. 'Me? No. Unlike Henry, I have no intention of running my head into that particular noose. Though I did get close to it once.'

The bitterness was still there, lacing the forced casualness of his words with acid. Folly hardly dared breathe, willing him to go on. There was a long pause, in which she became aware once more of the noise of the rotors overhead, and the grey, glinting surface of the Thames so far below. She could feel, rather than see, the tension building in his shoulders and arms.

Folly felt her heart go out to him. 'You gave her roses,' she whispered, hardly knowing where the thought had come from.

Luke gave another short laugh, and this time all the amusement had been eaten away, leaving only the acid. 'Roses, chocolates, jewellery, my heart on a platter—I gave Cherith everything except what she really wanted. I was intoxicated with her—and she played me like a fish on a line. Just like your precious Anne did to Henry. Except that in my case there was no need to wait for seven years. Only just as long as it took to get a licence.'

A cold sensation crept over Folly's heart. 'But. . .but you said you weren't married.'

Luke didn't seem to hear the fear in her voice. If he had he might have wondered. . . As she was beginning to wonder. But he was too tied up in his own remembered pain.

'I'm not,' he said grimly. 'But only because when we turned up at the solicitor's to work out the marriage settlement—her idea, not mine—she realised for the first time that I wasn't as rich as she thought. I was just building up my first business then, and a thing like that is a bit like riding a roller-coaster—you need all the speed you can collect on the downhill runs to take you over the next hump. I could afford to spend freely enough on a personal level—which was what confused her, I suppose. But taking out big sums would have been commercial suicide.'

'So what happened?'

'She walked out on me.' His voice was carefully expressionless. 'The last thing I heard was that she'd gone to America and married some newspaper magnate twice her age. So you can hardly expect me to share your rose-tinted spectacles when it comes to marriage.'

Folly knew she was taking a risk, but she had to say something. 'Luke, you can't condemn an entire institution because of one bad experience,' she ventured at last. 'Just because you were unlucky unlucky——'

But her companion shook his head. 'It's people like your parents who are lucky, it seems to me, not the other way around. Why should marriages work? People want different things; men and women want different things. Even if Cherith had been genuinely in love with me, how long do you thing we'd have stayed together? She was ambitious, and I liked that—but if we'd been married her ambitions and mine would have clashed at every turn.'

'But if you'd loved each other ——?'

'You're a romantic, Folly. Well, so am I—but I'm a realist, too. I've had to accept that the kind of woman who attracts me isn't the kind to sit at home having babies and darning my socks. And that's the kind who would bore me stiff within the week.' He smiled wryly. 'Two egos into one don't go, Folly. Ever since Cherith, I've vowed that I'd just take love as it comes—and as it goes. I'm just not the marrying kind.'

'And if a woman wanted to marry you?' Her tone was guarded. But she had to know. . .

Luke shot her a sideways glance. 'Then she wouldn't want me enough,' he said flatly. 'I can't pretend it hasn't happened once or twice. But I've never been tempted to change my mind.'

Because you've never met the right woman. . . she wanted to say. But however true it was, Folly had a feeling that that was one platitude that Luke Hunter didn't want to hear. In fact, given the bitterness the memory of Cherith still evoked, she wondered why he'd decided to confide in her at all. And came to the uncomfortable conclusion that it might have been a warning. . .

If so, then, having delivered it, he didn't seem anxious to continue the subject. 'I thought we could run up the river as far as Richmond or Kew,' he said, changing the subject abruptly. He fished out a brightly coloured map and handed it over. 'That way I can show you Buckingham Palace and the rest of the sights from the air. And maybe another time we can explore at ground level.'

'That sounds fine.' But the afternoon sunshine seemed less bright, and Folly had to battle to keep up her side of the conversation. A wholly unreasonable disappointment was souring her pleasure in the trip.

'Oh, Folly—you fool,' she muttered to herself under cover of the still-deafening noise of the rotors. But however much she told herself that Luke Hunter's matrimonial intentions were no business of hers, the feeling persisted.

She had met Luke Hunter only a few days earlier. She knew almost nothing about him. And yet, like Anne Boleyn all those centuries before her, she knew she was in imminent danger of losing her head. . .

CHAPTER FIVE

By the time Luke's driver delivered them back to the flat, Folly had managed to recapture most of her earlier carefree enthusiasm. Nothing had ever been able to keep her down for long—another advantage of her Arian birth-sign, her mother would have insisted. And Luke seemed to have recovered from the bitterness her innocent remark had triggered. Although the memory of their near-quarrel still lurked somewhere at the back of Folly's mind, the forefront of her attention had been much more pleasantly occupied.

So pleasantly, in fact, that now she could hardly bear for it to be over. So when he turned to her casually in the car, and suggested that they call in at his house for some tea before they parted, Folly found herself leaping on the suggestion with almost indecent haste. 'Oh, yes—I'd love to,' she accepted impulsively, then blushed as she realised how eager she must have sounded. 'I mean—not if you're busy, of course. And I'd rather have coffee than tea. . .'

But Luke was smiling. 'I think we can manage that.' He leant forward and spoke to the driver. 'But it's been a long day for Sam, so if you don't mind I'll send him home. I can send you back by taxi.'

He smiled again, his eyes hooding as he looked at her. Luke the hunter. . .Folly felt a thrill of anticipation, mingled with fear. Perhaps she shouldn't have accepted his invitation. But he was speaking again. 'Unless you'd rather I brought him in as chaperon?

Normally my housekeeper would be there, but it's her weekend off.'

The reference to her childish behaviour the previous night made Folly blush again, but she couldn't deny she deserved the gentle teasing. How stupid she had been! A man like Luke had no need to force his attentions on unwilling women—and he had nothing at all in common with her ex-fiancé. Tony had been weak—and, in his weakness, only too ready to betray her.

But Luke was different. Whatever hurts he had suffered in the past, with his Leo open-heartedness, he was one of nature's true romantics. She could imagine him picking out the blooms, thinking of her, his large, flamboyant writing looping across the card. . . Although they had known each other such a short time, she could sense that he cared about her. And she knew more and more clearly that she was beginning to care about him. In a very special way. . .

But that was for the future. Now, all that mattered was that she was following him up the stairs to an elegant Georgian town house. The day wasn't over, after all. And perhaps, when he said goodbye, he would 'kiss her properly' again. . .

As she stepped through the door Folly felt something inside her twist in delicious anticipation. But then the full force of Luke's home hit her straight between the eyes. And for a few moments everything else was forgotten.

Outside, the house was a model of classical restraint. But inside, it glowed with colour, and warmth, and life. The thick carpet beneath their feet was a glowing scarlet, and the high walls of the hallway were hung with modern tapestries—abstract compilations of brilliant colours that burned like fire.

Nothing could have been less in keeping with the architect's original intentions. It was as if someone had decided to repaint the Parthenon in pillar-box red. Luke saw her look of half-outraged surprise, and grinned.

'What do you think of it? The original stuff had all been ripped out years ago, so when I moved in I thought I'd go to town on the redecoration. I can't see the point of living in a mausoleum, just because it's "in period".'

'I can see that,' Folly said faintly. 'Those tapestries are amazing.'

He looked pleased. 'Actually, the woman who did them was a sort of protegée of mine. Unknown then, of course, but I knew she had talent. Now she's one of the top textile artists in the country.'

Folly winced as a pang of jealousy shot through her. It didn't take much imagination to supply another word in place of 'protegée'. Particularly if the woman was as flamboyant as her work.

But Luke didn't seem to notice. 'There's some more of her stuff through here in the living-room,' he called, beckoning from the end of the passage. 'She designed them for me specially. I told her I wanted something I could look at on days when it was too hot to have a fire.'

And, following him into the spacious room, Folly could see exactly how faithfully the artist had carried out her patron's—her lover's?—wishes. One wall was taken up by a great open fireplace, more suggestive of a baronial hall than a Georgian living-room. And another by a vast flame-coloured tapestry that almost flickered with heat. She wouldn't have been surprised to see the wall behind it char and burn.

'Effective, isn't it?' Luke was obviously enjoying the

effect his 'lair' was having on her. He gestured towards a golden-yellow sofa. 'Make yourself comfortable, Folly. I just want to see if there are any messages.'

He walked over to a small table at one side of the room, and started to fiddle with what Folly guessed must be an answering machine. The whirring sound of a tape rewinding at high speed confirmed her guess.

As she settled down into the squashy leather upholstery of the nest-like sofa she listened with half an ear to the voices on the tape, each caller seemingly convinced that disaster would intervene if Luke didn't call them back immediately. After the first, it occurred to her to wonder if she ought to offer to leave. But her host's calm demeanour as he scribbled a few notes and went on to the next call calmed her fears. Evidently Luke's own assessment of the problem's urgency was somewhat different from the caller's own.

One voice followed another, and she had almost stopped listening altogether when a sudden difference jerked her back to avid attention.

'Hello, Luke?' The new voice was a woman's—despite the unusual depth of tone, there was no doubt at all about that. It was a smooth, musical and utterly feminine voice, and Folly felt a surge of primitive jealousy.

'Luke—I need to talk to you. Phone me, will you?' The click that followed showed that this caller hadn't felt the need to leave careful details of where she might be contacted. Or even a name. . .Obviously it was someone that Luke knew very well.

But however well he knew the owner of the voice, Folly was relieved to see that Luke wasn't rushing to answer her summons. 'Nothing that can't wait,' he said cheerfully as he reset the machine. 'Now, I'll get you that coffee—only before that there's something I've been waiting to do all day.'

Before Folly could take in what was happening, Luke had crossed the room in a few strides and almost thrown himself on to the sofa. She felt his arms snake round her waist and before she could gain a purchase on the yielding upholstery he had pulled her close to his side. His mouth nuzzled the dark hair that fell across her neck.

'I don't know how I've kept my hands off you,' he murmured, as his lips found the tender skin below her ear. 'You don't know what you do to me, Folly.'

One hand strayed upwards to her breast, and the gentle touch of his fingers on the hardening tip sent liquid shivers down her spine. She moaned, and felt, rather than heard, his sigh of response against her skin. 'Or perhaps you do.' The words caressed her, teased her. 'Perhaps you feel the same. . .' His cheek was rough against the smoothness of her skin. 'I think you do, Folly. Don't you?'

She said nothing, but only arched back against the soft leather, lost in the tantalising, agonising pleasure of his hands—a pleasure that lit a fire deep inside her, but did nothing to quench it. But he whispered again, demanding her response.

'Say it, Folly. You feel it too. You want me. . .'

'Yes.' The admission was torn from her. But, however much her body yearned for submission, to let her will melt away in the pleasure Luke's expert hands could give her, still in the background of her mind was a sense of holding something back. At first she couldn't think why. But then it came to her.

His expert hands. . .Yes, that was it. Luke was an expert lover in every sense. He knew exactly how to touch her—how to stir her. But how had he learned that expertise? In other women's arms... She thought of Cherith, and the creator of the fire-tapestries. And the woman on the phone. No doubt they had all felt this melting ecstasy.

And now it was her turn. But for how long? The pleasure she had been feeling turned sour, and she pushed him away.

'What's the matter, Folly?' Luke gripped her gently by the shoulders. 'What are you afraid of? You've admitted that you want me. And I didn't think that you were into playing games.'

'I'm not.' Her voice was tight. 'But this isn't a game—or not to me. I've only known you a few days, Luke, and I don't go in for casual sex.'

She half expected him to be angry, but he seemed amused rather than annoyed. 'If and when I make love to you, the last thing it will be is "casual sex".' He stroked her cheek with one rough thumb. 'There's nothing casual about the way I feel about you, Folly. That's why...' The tempo of his caresses quickened, making it difficult for her to think.

'Why you felt you had to warn me off?' Folly struggled to keep her brain clear. 'Why else did you tell me about Cherith—except to make it clear that nothing was on offer here except a little temporary pleasure? That sounds like casual sex to me.'

'Then you're wrong.' His temper was beginning to rise now, she could feel it. And see it, flashing gold in his eyes. 'I don't know why I told you that story—it isn't one I'm very proud of. Except that I thought you'd understand—and perhaps I did think that you had a right to know why I feel the way I do about...about anything permanent.' It was as if he couldn't bring himself to say the word 'marriage'. 'Not to warn you off—but just to warn you. Wedding bells and roses aren't for me, Folly. That wouldn't bother some women. . .'

'But you think it might bother me.' Folly finished the sentence for him in a flat voice that she hardly recognised as being her own.

'That's right.' He looked at her straight in the eyes. 'And it does, doesn't it? You scare me, Folly—you're not like the other women I've known. You don't know the rules. And I'm afraid of hurting you.'

It was a moment of decision. Folly knew that if she said 'yes'—if she walked out now—this strangely disturbing relationship would be over. He wouldn't follow her. They scarcely knew each other, after all—despite the mysterious chemistry that seemed to pull them together.

She would get over him. In a few months' time she might hardly remember his name. Whereas if she stayed. . .

She had only to make the decision. And inside her head the words she longed to speak hammered at her brain. I don't know what matters any more, she wanted to shout. I only know that I want you—all of you. And that I'm horribly jealous of all the women you've probably had in the past. I'm jealous of Cherith, and of the woman who made these tapestries, and the voice on the phone. And what I hate even more is the thought that I'm just the next number on your list. That one day I'll just be history, like the rest. . .

The words rang so clear in her head that she could hardly believe she hadn't spoken them aloud. But some sense of self-preservation held her back. If she wanted Luke she would have to play by his rules.

And she did want him. Summoning her courage, Folly looked him squarely in the face. 'I'm not made of paper, Luke.' Her voice wavered, but then she caught it, and went on. 'I'm a grown woman. I can make my own choices.'

'I know that.' He pulled her closer, and she felt the stirrings of electricity flicker between them again. But it was too soon—and too dangerous. Her feelings were still in turmoil. Feeling her resistance, Luke drew away.

She had herself under better control now. 'And besides,' she added briskly, 'this would be a bad time for me to be getting involved with anything serious. Building up the Rose Bowl is going to take all my energies over the next year or so. So you needn't worry, Luke. I'm not any more interested in anything permanent than you are. But I'd like to see you again, when we can make time. So why don't we just let things develop at their own pace?'

Folly was proud of this speech—but Luke didn't seem quite as pleased by it as Folly had expected. 'That's fine by me,' he responded a little gruffly. 'I just wanted to be sure...Now what about that coffee? That is, if you're sure you can make time?'

But, as she opened her mouth to accept, Folly suddenly realised that she was close to the limit of her endurance. She needed to get away and think things through, before the emotional burden toppled her control. So instead she shook her head. 'I'd better go, Luke. I didn't realise how tired I am—and I've got a lot to do tomorrow. But it's been a marvellous day.'

'Then I'll see you again.'

It wasn't a question, but a statement. And the certainty of it gave her the strength to smile. 'I should hope so. You haven't solved my business problems yet.'

He grinned. 'I'll phone you.'

Folly held up her face to be kissed. And, although

the meeting of their lips had none of the searching hunger that they had shared before, there was something in the touch that reassured her. And as he walked her out to hail a taxi she felt a strange lightness invade her heart.

'Well—for a business disaster waiting to happen, you seem to have come off remarkably unscathed.'

Looking at Luke across the wide, modern desk that separated them, Folly felt one of the knots in her stomach untie itself. It wasn't the first time Luke had contacted her since their sight seeing expedition—the flowers that by now she was coming to expect had arrived promptly next day, and with them a handwritten note—but it was the first time that she had heard his voice. Even the call asking her to see him at his office had been made by a secretary.

So her relief at the friendly, bantering tone sent her spirits sky-high, and at first she hardly took in the news he was giving her. Then it sank in, and another knot untwined. 'You mean, it's all right? There's no problem with the shop?'

But this seemed to be further than Luke was prepared to go. 'Let's say that there's good news and bad news,' he corrected cautiously. 'You are the leaseholder—or will be, when the sale is completed. Which is a good start. There's nothing wrong with the terms of the agreement you signed. And the price you paid seems to be fair enough—even taking the bad news into account. Your Miss Philimore may be a sharp operator, but it seems she's basically honest. Maybe your parents should have christened you "Lucky", instead of "Folly".'

'"Eutyche". . .' Folly frowned consideringly, then shook her head. 'I think I like Aphrosyne better. But what do you mean, "taking the bad news into account"? What bad news, Luke? Is it serious?'

She had expected an immediate 'no', and felt a moment's panic when Luke failed at first to respond. Surely he wouldn't be joking if something was seriously wrong. . .and he had called her 'Lucky'. . .But his face was serious now, and he seemed to be taking an inordinate interest in the grain of his desktop.

'I can't tell you that, Folly,' he said at last, raising his head again to look her squarely in the eye. It gave her the uncomfortable feeling of being turned inside out for better examination. And she wasn't sure whether or not she had passed.

She looked away as Luke's voice went slowly on. 'I can't tell you, because I don't know. A lot will depend on you. It's nothing unexpected. But we managed to track down your kindly vendor's accountant, and persuade them to bring those accounts up to date.'

'And?' His reluctance was infuriating.

Luke shrugged. 'As I said, nothing unexpected. Ever since the expansion of that department store, the Rose Bowl's sales have been going down. In fact, in the last quarter the shop made a net loss. It's in a bad way, Folly. No doubt about that.'

She felt her mouth open, but no sounds came out. 'And that's lucky?' she managed at last. 'The business I've just bought is on the rocks, and you tell me that's lucky?'

'I said it depended on you.' He gave her another of those inquisitorial looks. 'If the business had been in good heart it would have cost you a great deal more. Didn't it surprise you that you could afford such a prime location?'

'I don't know—I suppose so. But I hadn't looked at many other places. And it all happened so quickly. . .'

'That's not surprising. My guess is that your vendor was scared that if she waited much longer it would be impossible to sell the place as a going concern and she would lose out completely on fittings and goodwill. So she advertised it at a knock-down price, and then invented a competitive bid to hurry you into signing on the dotted line. The price you paid was fair enough, but the net result is that if the business fails now it's you who'll stand the loss.'

Folly couldn't understand the note of satisfaction in his voice. 'Oh, good,' she said sarcastically. 'Well, at least it's nothing serious.'

Luke shook his head. 'There are two sides to every situation, Folly. What I said is quite true—if the business fails then you'll lose out. But the converse is that if you can make it work you'll have bought a fair lease on a prime site that you could never have afforded in the ordinary way. It could be the best deal you ever made. If you had the additional capital to go all-out for a new start I'd say it was almost a certainty. But I assume you haven't?'

Folly shook her head despondently. 'It took virtually the whole of my grandmother's legacy to buy out the lease—all I've got left is a bit to keep me going until I start to show a profit. And now you tell me that might take forever. . .'

'And your parents couldn't help out?'

This time the answer was decisive. 'I wouldn't ask them. They probably do have a bit put away—but not enough that they can afford to risk it.'

'Then there are only two alternatives. Either you manage without capital—which won't be easy, believe me. Or you raise it outside.'

'Outside? What, you mean, from a bank?' Folly looked at him doubtfully. Even her financial naïveté couldn't conceal that she was hardly in the best position to inspire the generosity of bankers.

But that wasn't what Luke had in mind. For a second, his eyes gleamed gold as he leant back into his chair. 'I wasn't thinking of a bank, Folly. I was thinking of me.'

For a moment she could hardly take it in. 'You? But why ——?'

He shrugged. 'Because it's good business—for someone who doesn't mind a gamble, and could afford to take a loss. I'm not offering you this for the sake of your pretty brown eyes, Folly—it's a business proposition, pure and simple. No strings attached—on either side.'

'I see,' she said slowly. But her mind was racing. How typical it was of Luke to make his position so crystal-clear, drawing the line almost brutally in his determination that she shouldn't make any personal conclusions from his offer.

But there was something else. . . Again she had the feeling that he was testing her. But whether it meant she passed or failed, Folly knew that there was only one answer she could make. 'I'm, sorry, Luke.' She saw a look of surprise pass over his features. So he had expected her to accept. . .But that only hardened her resolve. 'The Rose Bowl is my business, Luke—it's my baby. I can't share it—not if there's any chance of making it on my own.'

She couldn't say to him, if once I let you in you'll take the whole thing over—and me as well. But that was what she meant. However well-meaning Luke Hunter might be, she had no intention of letting herself be steamrollered by him—in business or anything else.

'I'm not ungrateful, Luke,' she hurried on. 'And I know you could give me lots of good advice on how to make a success of it. I'm probably being a fool to turn you down. But surely you can understand? How would you have felt if someone with a hundred times your experience had tried to buy into one of your early ventures?'

There was a long silence, during which Folly almost held her breath. Had she ruined everything? But at last Luke smiled—and the warmth of it surprised her. Was it possible that he had actually wanted her to turn his offer down? But that didn't make sense. If he hadn't wanted to invest in the Rose Bowl he could simply never have suggested it...

But, whatever his real feelings, at least he wasn't angry. 'I see what you mean,' he said slowly. Folly let out a long breath of relief. 'But you do realise that you'll be doing it the hard way? It's a gamble, Folly—and it will need a lot of commitment to bring the odds round to your favour.'

There was something in his voice that gave her hope. 'But you do think there's a chance?'

He nodded. 'I think there could be. Unless she's been fiddling the books—and my accountant doesn't think so—the profits your Miss Philimore has been turning in seem on the low side for a site like that. My theory would be that the place has been seriously mismanaged. And that means that there is scope for improving the position just by doing it right.'

'Oh.' Folly felt suddenly and painfully aware of the fact that the only qualification she had to run a shop was an unfinished college course and a healthy belief that you could do most things if you tried. 'But do you think I can do that?'

Luke grinned, and suddenly she knew it was going to be all right. 'No, I don't suppose you can,' he said bluntly. 'You haven't the experience. But I could. And I'm damn well going to try.'

'So what do I do next?' Folly wasn't sure if her growing feeling of euphoria was due to Luke's excitement about the Rose Bowl's possibilities—or the commitment to the future of their relationship that his willingness to help her implied. Either way, she was looking forward to putting their plans into action with a relish she hadn't felt since the first heady moment of signing the lease.

'What we need now is information,' he told her, leaning forward across the desk to make his point. Folly made a note on the pad in front of her, but she was more conscious of the fact that their heads were so close than of any particular significance in what she was writing. She could feel his breath on her cheek, and smell the faint warm scent of his skin. He didn't wear aftershave—she liked that. He smelt only of soap, and something disturbingly male. . .

'So you need to keep in with the present owner,' he went on. 'Don't let her know what you've found out, or she'll only clam up. You need to know everything about the way she buys, the way she sells, the way she checks up that that girl who works for her hasn't got her fingers in the till—everything about the way she runs that business. And especially how she monitors waste—with a perishable product like flowers the waste percentage could be crucial.'

Folly nodded. That made sense, and fitted in with what she remembered from college business lectures. 'I'll be going in regularly until I take over; at least part-time,' she said eagerly. 'Miss Philimore's already agreed to that. I thought I'd have to take time off to look for somewhere to live, but, thanks to you, I can leave that till I'm settled. So I should be able to make it every day.'

He smiled again, in a way that made her heart turn over. 'Not every day, I hope. I had it on my schedule to see quite a lot of you over the next few weeks, Folly. Purely in a business capacity, of course.'

But his eyes belied his words, and Folly felt a new happiness rise within her. Nevertheless, she tried to keep her voice cool. Although he might have decided to forget the way they had clashed at their last meeting, she had no doubt that Luke's misgivings were still there. It wouldn't do to risk triggering them again. 'Of course.' Her joking tone matched his almost to perfection. 'Purely business.'

'Like Saturday, for instance? We still have to complete your familiarisation course. And there's another restaurant I know which is ideal for working dinners.'

'That sounds. . .very businesslike.'

'Then I'd better get on with running my own business. But don't forget to start thinking about ways you could expand, where you wouldn't be competing directly with other outlets like that department store.' Luke stood up abruptly, pushing his chair away. 'I've got a couple of books on marketing that you could read. And I run occasional training seminars for my own people. We're about due for one—I might bring you in on it.'

He moved over to the other side of the office and had begun searching through a well-stocked bookshelf when the phone on his desk rang close by Folly's hand. Without thinking, she picked it up.

'Hello, Luke?'

It was the voice she had heard on Luke's home answering machine, and Folly felt the suffocating jealousy rise up to choke her agan. 'Just a moment,' she said stiffly. 'Luke, it's for you.'

He took the receiver and perched on the desk by Folly's chair. His leg swung so close that the smooth black cloth brushed against her breast, setting the nerve-endings tantalisingly on edge. She felt her nipple stiffen in expectation.

But Luke didn't seem to notice the effect he was having on her. 'Hello, Lexy. What? Right. Yes, of course. No problem.' Folly stared fixedly at the desk in an attempt not to listen to the one-sided conversation. But by the time Luke replaced the receiver she had an angry idea of what was going to come next.

And she was right. 'I'm sorry, Folly; something's come up. Business, I'm afraid. So the weekend's out.' He pulled out a leather-bound diary and scanned the pages. 'I could make tomorrow evening for dinner, though. We'll have to do our sightseeing some other time.'

For a moment Folly was tempted to refuse. It was the 'no problem' that had rankled. That and that voice. . . But then her common sense took over, and she dredged up a smile.

'That would be fine, Luke. Tomorrow it is.' If she was trying to impress Luke with her willingness to play by his rules, acting like a jealous child over what was undoubtedly a business phone call was hardly the way to begin.

But that didn't mean she had to like it. Or the owner of the voice.

Which was really just as well.

CHAPTER SIX

'ARIES and Leo—I told you there'd be sparks.'

Her mother sounded almost *pleased*, Folly thought in exasperation. Just because her astrological theories were being proved right. But where was her sympathy for her daughter, caught in the middle of this conflict? Folly was beginning to wish she had never mentioned that she was seeing Luke, but her straightforward nature made it difficult to conceal something that was so far to the forefront of her mind. She had kept her secret for two weeks—but today it had somehow slipped out.

'It's not Aries and Leo that are the problem, Mum,' she said impatiently. 'It's Folly Taylor and Luke Hunter. And I don't see that it helps to blame it on the stars. Presumably a twelfth or so of the population are Leos, and they aren't all self-opinionated, domineering, power-mad ——'

'Strong-willed, generous, reliable, principled and creative? Yes, that sounds like a Leo. Everyone has the defects of their qualities, darling—or is it the qualities of their defects? Anyway, you know what I mean.'

'Do I?' Folly was in no mood to have Luke Hunter's behaviour excused—on the grounds of his star sign or anything else. She had just come away from yet another meeting in which he had been waxing expansive about what *he* could do with *her* business. And, even more difficult to cope with, she had a suspicion that most of his suggestions were right. . . But that didn't mean she had to like the way he treated her like some sort of assistant.

'Of course you do, dear,' her mother said patiently. 'It's just that, being an Aries, you're too stubborn to admit it. Which just goes to prove what I'm saying. You can't be single-minded, energetic, enterprising and direct without occasionally erring on the side of pig-headedness, foolhardiness and bad temper.'

For someone so vague in everyday life, Folly thought resentfully, her mother had a startlingly good memory for the facts connected with her favourite hobby-horse. 'I am not stubborn, Mother. And I am *not* in a bad temper.'

'Oh, yes, you are—you called me "Mother",' the voice on the other end of the line retorted cheerfully. 'And I should know, having brought you up for twenty-odd years. But that's my point, you see—it's always a lot easier to see other people's faults than your own. Especially when you love them. I don't know why they say that love is blind—I was always *very* keenly aware of all your father's little defects.'

Her fond tone belied her words—but, in any case, Folly hardly heard the last half of her mother's speech. But although she opened her mouth to make it quite clear to her infuriating parent that she was not, never would be, and never wanted to even think about being in love with Luke Hunter, somehow the words wouldn't come. And instead, all she could hear was a wailing noise that she hardly recognised as her own voice.

'Oh, Mum—what am I going to do? It's ridiculous— I've only known him for a few weeks. And, quite apart from anything else, I'm far too busy to have time for falling in love. If you had any idea how much I've got to do before I take over the shop ——'

'But he's helping you with that, isn't he?'

Her daughter gave a hollow groan at the idea of Luke 'helping' to do anything. Taking over, yes—organising, yes again. But *helping*. . .

Mrs Agathangelou ignored it. 'And as for how long you've known him, you can hardly expect me to tell you that that makes any difference. I knew your Papa was the one as soon as I saw him. So why shouldn't you?'

Folly shook her head, then realised that the gesture wouldn't travel too well over the telephone wires and did her best to translate it into words. 'Oh, I don't know, Mum. But it was different for you and Papa. For a start, he presumably felt the same way. You both knew you wanted to get married. Whereas Luke's made it absolutely clear that he's not interested in anything permanent.' Keeping her voice as detached as possible, she gave her mother a brief—and heavily expurgated—resumé of what Luke had told her the day of their sightseeing trip.

'He actually told you that?' The older woman seemed to find the story intriguing rather than depressing. 'And almost as soon as you'd met? Oh, but darling—that's very hopeful. After all—he'd hardly bother telling you that unless something had put it into his mind. If you ask me, he's halfway to being in love with you already. He sounds to me like a man who's running scared. . .'

Running scared. . . The words stuck in Folly's mind, coming back to her next morning as she sat at the Rose Bowl's work-table, preparing roses for conditioning by crushing the tips of their stems with a heavy mallet. It was a satisfying sort of job, good for working off frustrations—of which she seemed currently to have rather more than her fair share. And it also had the benefit of requiring very little concentration, leaving her thoughts free to roam.

On the surface, nothing seemed less likely than that Luke Hunter should be scared of anything. But somehow her mother's words had struck a chord. Because, however much his words might deny that he cared for her, his actions spoke differently. There were the lavish bouquets, with their personal messages, that arrived after every date—and his sensitivity in not pushing their relationship too fast.

Luke hadn't visited her at the flat again, nor invited her back to his house. And, although one part of her found it deeply frustrating, at another level Folly was grateful for his restraint. With Tony it had been easy to make facile decisions about 'waiting for marriage'. With Luke the situation was far more complex.

The marriage she had assumed naïvely would be the end of every serious relationship now seemed a very distant—if not unreachable—shore. Whereas Luke was very near, and the feelings he aroused in her were like an undertow, pulling her down. If—when—he decided he had waited long enough, she was far from certain what her response would be.

Because although she kept a guard on her tongue when she was with him, determined not to risk another quarrel, she had had to stop pretending to herself. Whether Luke Hunter wanted to know it or not, she had fallen in love with him. And she was well past the point at which she might have stopped her headlong dive into that dizzying state.

She found she could sit at work in the Rose Bowl, her hands occupied as they were now, while in her head she relived the moments she had spent with Luke; his hands caressing her; his mouth on hers.

That was the real world. And even the shrill ill-temper of the proprietor and the lackadaisical attitude of Lisa, her assistant, had no power to break through the shell that a moment's introspection could weave round her. Although Folly knew her thoughts should have been occupied in absorbing a myriad pieces of information about the running of the shop, somehow, inevitably, they would slip away. And she would find herself remembering. . .Only to wake up back to reality with a small, secret smile on her lips.

Like now, when Miss Philimore's genteel voice broke in on her reverie. 'My dear, since you will be taking over next week, I think it is about time I explained our system for dealing with our more *special* customers. This is the book where we keep their records, and of course it must always be kept securely under lock and key when not in use.'

Folly hastily rearranged her face into an expression of businesslike interest. On Luke's advice, she hadn't mentioned any of his misgivings about the deal she had struck, and the woman now behaved towards her with a patronising graciousness that Folly found intensely irritating.

'Special customers? Oh, you mean, local business accounts like Mr Hunter's?'

Miss Philimore inclined her head in agreement. 'Mainly—and of course Mr Hunter is one of our biggest. But we do have a number of private accounts as well, where people buy a lot of flowers and prefer to pay their bills once a month.' She gave an unpleasant smirk. 'And we also have one or two gentlemen who just like the convenience of being able to place a "standing order", as it were, for their wives' anniversaries and birthdays. That way they don't have to worry about remembering every year.'

Folly nodded, trying not to show her distaste, even though she privately thought that any man who couldn't be bothered to remember his wife's birthday didn't deserve to be married. Poor women, receiving a gift with so little thought behind it! But business was business—and Miss Philimore was busy explaining that the service attracted an additional fee, as well as guaranteeing repeat business for year after year.

'As you can see, Miss Taylor, the accounts are listed alphabetically, with any special instructions and the names and addresses of any regular orders.' She leafed through the pages of the file. 'That way they don't need to repeat the information every time they ring. And we have a classification code of "A" to "E" to indicate the price required. So "E" would just be a nice mixed bunch of seasonal flowers, where as "A" would give scope for something really special. Our set prices for the different categories are listed here, at the front of the book.'

Folly had to admit that it seemed an efficient enough system. All the florist had to do was check through the dates listed in the book every afternoon to see if there were any standing orders for the next day. 'What about cards to put with the orders?' she asked. 'Do we write those ourselves?'

Her instructress beamed her approval. 'A very good question, my dear. I can see that you'll soon be picking up the reins. Yes, of course most people are quite happy for us to write the cards, in which case the appropriate message will be noted down in the book. Or a simple "Best Wishes" will suffice. But other customers prefer to write the messages themselves, for more of a personal touch. So in that case. . .'

She bent down, with a perceptible creaking of corsetry, and rummaged under the counter, emerging with a plastic card-index file. 'In that case, we ask them to write the cards at the time of order, and we store them in here,' she explained a little breathlessly, but with obvious pride. 'Each is *most* carefully marked in pencil with the names of sender and recipient, of course.'

She laughed, a little coyly. 'It would hardly be the thing to risk confusing them. And I always keep the box securely locked, and I put the cards in the envelopes myself and stick them down *securely*. Then I can safely leave Lisa to make up the flowers when she has time. I'm afraid she has a most irreverent attitude— and some of our gentlemen have quite a *wide* circle of acquaintances, so of course we must be able to offer complete discretion. . .'

'Oh, yes—I can see that.' Folly could just imagine. No doubt some of the same 'gentlemen' who couldn't be bothered to remember their wives' birthdays were equally glad to be relieved of the responsibility of remembering their mistresses'. She felt touched with a momentary bitterness. It was the sort of arrangement she could imagine suiting Tony very well. Why couldn't men just be faithful?

But then, most men were, she reminded herself. it was hardly fair to tar them all with Tony's brush. And she carried on with the arrangement she was making, cheerfully unaware of how great a change in attitude that charitable thought represented. Otherwise it might have occurred to her to wonder just what had happened since her arrival in London to so raise her jaundiced opinion of the whole male sex. . .

It was half-past eight on Thursday evening. And Luke Hunter was late. For about the seventh time Folly walked over to the vase on the mantelpiece which held the flowers he had sent her that morning. Picking up the card that had come with them, she read:

> Looking forward to this evening, darling. See you at eight.

Well, there wasn't much doubt about that. She had the time right—he just wasn't here. And she was beginning to wonder if he was ever coming. . .

Fifteen minutes later she had almost decided he wasn't. It was made all the more infuriating by the fact that she had dressed with more than usual care, splashing out far more than she could afford on a red silk jersey creation from an expensive boutique. Just because he'd said he would like to see her in red. And now ——

But she had to be fair. Forcing herself to sit down, she racked her imagination for excuses that might explain his absence.

He was ill—except that how many diseases came on so quickly that a man could send you flowers in the morning and by dinner be incapable of lifting the telephone? He'd had an accident—yes, that was more likely. Only somehow she couldn't imagine Luke Hunter being delayed by anything as feeble as stepping in front of a taxi. He seemed far too competent for life to catch him out in so trivial a way.

A business disaster, then? That was possible. For a few moments she imagined the scene as dark-suited managers with grim faces waited with bated breath for the one man who could step in and save the company. . .

But, no matter how she imagined the scene, there was always one flaw. There was always a telephone somewhere, on a desk or on a wall. She toyed briefly with a picture of Luke lying, bound and kidnapped, in some distant, cut-off retreat, but it didn't ring true. This was London, for goodness' sake. A centre of global communications. There was always a telephone.

So why the hell didn't he ring her?

She walked back to the mantelpiece again and stared at the card as if she could contact its writer by clairvoyance. If only she had seen him come into the shop—but she always seemed to miss him. In fact, she had wondered if perhaps he deliberately avoided visiting the shop when he knew she was there, to make sure the flowers he sent her retained their air of surprise.

The flowers had probably been ordered soon after the Rose Bowl opened, and that morning she had taken time off to buy the dress that was now causing her indecision. So she had arrived late, to find a scene of near chaos, with a shopful of customers and Miss Philimore departed suffering from the current strain of summer flu.

Lisa had been fully occupied explaining to a rather elderly lady why she couldn't pick out the exact blooms that were to be delivered to her daughter-in-law in New Zealand. So it hadn't occurred to Folly to ask her assistant if Luke had been in.

And besides, although the owner of the Rose Bowl presumably realised that she was receiving almost as many flowers as she sold, Folly was fairly sure that Lisa knew nothing of her relationship with Luke Hunter. Luke's sense of humour ensured that the flowers invariably came addressed to 'Aphrosyne Taylor-Agathangelou', whereas in the shop she was always plain 'Folly Taylor'. So even if Lisa made up the deliveries, there was no reason why she should make the connection.

Which was just as well. Folly didn't want to encourage the sort of speculation that would give rise to —

especially when she was so near to taking over as boss. But to know that he had been there, and she hadn't seen him. . .

Then her recollection of Miss Philimore's ailment put a new and comforting thought into Folly's mind. Hadn't Lisa mentioned laryngitis as one of the symptoms? Yes—in fact, she remembered thinking that a touch of it wouldn't do her assistant any harm. . . And the whole thing had apparently come on quite suddenly. So if Luke had contracted the same strain it might explain why he couldn't phone her ——

It was a possible explanation. But it didn't quite ring true. Folly stood up and resumed her pacing, practising in her head all the things she would say to Luke Hunter when he finally deigned to make contact.

But at that moment the phone perversely decided to break its vow of silence and ring—if 'ring' was quite the right word for the refined sound by which it alerted her to its sleekly Design-Centred presence. Folly hurled herself towards it, completely forgetting her intention to count to ten and act cool. But, when she picked it up and gasped a breathless 'hello', the voice that answered wasn't Luke at all.

'Is that Miss Taylor?' Although Folly had heard it only twice before, the low, mellifluous voice was instantly recognisable—and as immediately detestable. Folly felt the hairs on the back of her neck stand on end with irrational dislike. Something snapped inside her, and, almost before she knew what she was doing, she had hurled the elegant telephone away from her, yanking the socket from the wall.

How dared he? How dared he stand her up—and then get that woman to phone and make his excuses? Folly fanned her anger like a flame, trying desperately to burn out the suspicions that crowded into her mind.

This wasn't Tony, after all. This was Luke—and, if he had intended to break their date, it was highly unlikely that he would have sent her flowers to confirm it only that morning. . .But fear and anger tightened her throat almost to choking-point.

Folly was painfully aware that she was acting completely unreasonably. No doubt Luke would turn out to have good reason for breaking their date; no doubt there was an equally good reason why he hadn't rung her in person to apologise. If she could only have been sure. . .

But Luke was a man, after all. Like Tony. . . And with a grey sense of certainty she knew she could never be that sure ever again.

But by the next morning sleep had smoothed over the ragged edges of Folly's doubt. She was still angry with Luke—he had been thoughtless, and surprisingly insensitive. But she was beginning to realise that there was no real reason to leap to more worrying conclusions.

After all, the woman with the voice—what had Luke called her that day in his office? 'Lexy', that was right— was almost certainly some kind of employee of Luke's. That all fitted in with the theory that the reason for Luke's non-appearance must be some kind of business disaster. And there were a hundred reasons why he might have had to ask Lexy to make the phone call.

It was true that none of the ones that sprang to mind seemed particularly adequate to Folly, but then Luke probably hadn't even thought she might be jealous. And she herself had acted very childishly, which left the honours about even. She re-plugged the disconnected telephone, feeling almost guilty. The message Lexy had been going to pass on might have explained everything. He might even have been planning to meet her at the restaurant direct. . .

She owed him at least a chance to explain, and decided to drop into his offices on her way to the shop.

It was still well before nine when she pushed her way through the revolving doors of Lucas Sales, and Luke's employees were drifting in in ones and twos. But the efficient-looking woman who had manned the reception desk on Folly's previous visit was not yet at her post.

Folly glanced at her watch. If she waited much longer, she would be late at the shop, and as there was a good chance Lisa would be alone that was something she didn't really want to risk. She was about to turn away, when a voice behind her said tentatively, 'Do you need any help?'

The enquirer was a friendly, bubbly girl of about twenty-three. Folly vaguely remembered seeing her somewhere in the outer office when she had visited before, and turned to her gratefully.

'I really just wanted to see if Mr Hunter was available,' she said, trying to keep her voice casual. 'I believe he may have been trying to contact me. I know it's early, but I have to get to work ——'

'Oh, that's all right. He's bound to be in by now—he's always early. I'll take you up, shall I?' Without waiting for an answer, she led the way towards the lift.

Folly followed her guide, praying that the girl wouldn't ask why she wanted to see Luke Hunter, and trying to think up a good excuse in case she did. But the question didn't come. And a few moments later she was shown into the office she remembered from before.

Only this time it was empty. 'Oh, that's odd. Perhaps he's out today, although I thought. . . I'll ask around.'

The girl stuck her head out into the main office and called across the room. 'Does anyone know where Luke is? There's someone looking for him.'

The answer came almost immediately. 'They're out of luck, then. He's off on one of his jaunts with Sexy Lexy, and then they're going straight down to the country for the weekend. So I doubt if he'll be back in the office until Monday. Who is it wants him?'

The girl who had shown her in turned back to Folly with the question on her lips. But Folly shook her head. 'It doesn't matter,' she said grimly, only too aware that her white face showed that it mattered only too much. 'It was just a personal call. I'll contact him at home.' And, before she could fall victim to the tears of rage that threatened her, she stumbled past the startled girl towards the lift.

Once outside, she couldn't hold the storm off any longer. It was obvious that she couldn't go into the Rose Bowl until she had calmed down, so instead she started walking back towards the flat. Lisa would just have to cope for an hour or two. She needed a sit down, a cup of strong coffee, and a chance to get the whole thing in proportion.

But when she entered the little kitchen the first thing she saw was the flowers. An even more extravagant bouquet than usual lay waiting for her on the draining-board.

Folly's first thought was of delight, that Luke should want to apologise for breaking their date. Surely that must mean that there was a rational explanation to all that had happened?

Her second was a slight feeling of surprise that, if he was 'out on a jaunt', he should have been able to order flowers from the Rose Bowl. But, of course, she was being foolish. He must have ordered them by telephone when he'd found himself unable to contact her direct.

But then she saw his large, confident black writing on the card, and forgot her annoyance. He must have been in town after all. And he had probably expected to see her at the shop this morning, while she had been waiting impatiently at his office. What a muddle! She should have guessed that he would try to make contact.

Eagerly she tugged the card off the Cellophane wrapping—then stared at it in confusion.

> Thank you for a wonderful evening, Folly, darling.

It didn't make sense. Even as some kind of joke, it didn't make sense. Folly turned the card over and over in her hands, as if by her looking at it from another direction the words might mysteriously transpose themselves into the expected apology. It was definitely Luke's handwriting, and it couldn't even be that he had sent the flowers to the wrong address. Her name was clear enough.

What possible reason could a sane man have for thanking her for an evening that had never happened?

Then a mark on the back of the card caught her eye. It was nothing legible—just a pencil smudge, as if something had been written there and then rubbed out with a dirty eraser. But it jogged a memory somewhere, and she found herself examining it with a growing sense of unease.

And then it came to her. Of course—the other day at the Rose Bowl, when Miss Philimore had been demonstrating her system for dealing with 'standing orders'. The little card box with its pathetic collection of pre-written endearments, carefully labelled and dated in pencil, just waiting for their turn.

But that was for bored husbands, and businessmen

dating their secretaries. Surely it couldn't apply to her? But the longer she stared at that tiny betraying smudge, the more she realised that it was the only explanation that made any sense at all.

CHAPTER SEVEN

RATHER to Folly's surprise, Lisa seemed to have things well in hand by the time she had calmed down enough to return to the Rose Bowl. In fact, despite the fact that Friday was always their busiest day, the girl seemed to be enjoying herself.

She greeted Folly cheerfully. 'I must say, it's a lot better here without the old dragon breathing down my neck. I could almost get to like it.' She handed over a neatly wrapped 'mixed bunch' to one customer, with a chatty, 'Here you are, love,' and moved swiftly on to the next.

Folly dropped her handbag underneath the table and took the next in the queue. 'I'll give you a hand until the rush dies down and then I thought I'd get on with the account orders for tomorrow,' she said casually, but the girl gave her a strange look, and Folly had a nasty feeling that her voice wasn't as fully under control as she had thought. Lisa was very perceptive.

But if the girl had her suspicions she said nothing about them. 'Yeah, sure; I'll do today's stuff. Do you know where the cards and things are?'

Folly nodded. 'I think so.' Her hands were fully occupied, but her brain was still racing ahead. In what direction, she wasn't sure. What exactly would it mean if she did find her name on Luke Hunter's account? Perhaps nothing, except that his 'romantic gestures' had been rather more cold-blooded than she had thought—just as there might be some business explanation for their broken date and Luke's 'jaunt' with

Lexy. 'Sexy' Lexy, they had called her. But taken together. . .

But there was no point in speculating until she had some facts. Folly forced her mind back on to business. 'What happened about the orders you made up yesterday?'

As soon as the words were out she could have kicked herself. Of course the orders had gone out—she herself had been one of the recipients. How strange to think that Luke's calculating message had been lying here in the shop since the day before. All the time she had been waiting for him to call, it had been there. . .

Lisa nodded. 'I phoned the relief driver when I realised you weren't coming in. And I told him we might want him again this afternoon.'

Despite her preoccupation, Folly was impressed with her assistant's unexpected initiative. Perhaps without Miss Philimore's continual criticism she might become an asset to the shop. She certainly seemed to thrive on responsibility when she was given it.

'Thanks, Lisa. You've coped extremely well.' She saw the other girl redden with pleasure. Together they worked swiftly through the rest of the queue until at last the flow stopped and the little shop was empty.

Lisa settled down with the bulldog clip that held the current day's orders, and Folly picked up the accounts book. A workmanlike silence fell, broken only by the snip of scissors on stems, and the steady scratching of Folly's pencil as she scribbled out the orders for next day.

Some streak of reluctance stopped her from turning straight to Luke's page in the book. Instead, she set to stubbornly work her way through in alphabetical order, so that before long she had a small pile of pink order slips in front of her.

When she finally turned over a page and saw his name, it seemed oddly unreal.

> Lucas Sales Ltd—contact Mr L Hunter or secretary.

And underneath was a list of names and addresses—his regular clients, presumably. There were about twenty names; some with several dates beside them. Some were marked as regular orders, some as one-offs. He must send a lot of flowers—but then she knew that already.

Folly started to read down the list, but then her eye was caught by an emphatic message, scrawled across the page in capitals and underlined twice.

NEVER ROSES.

Cherith's betrayal had bitten deep, then—deeper even than Folly had realised. She had understood his reluctance to send roses to the women in his life, but Luke had gone further than that. He had actually taken the trouble of ruling them out for all his business contacts as well.

'I don't like the thorns...' She remembered how the temperature in the restaurant had dropped when she had made her unwitting gaffe. And felt a sudden surge of unwilling pity.

But just then Lisa looked up from the basket whose handle she was binding with ribbon, and laughed. 'Is that the gorgeous Mr Hunter?' she queried. 'If it is, it means what it says. And we don't dare forget it. I don't know what he's got against roses, but if you use even one in a bouquet he goes up the wall. Refuses to pay for it, too. I stuck some in once when we were a bit short and the old bat threatened to stop it out of my wages. Honestly, the scene he made, you'd have thought the world was about to come to an end. Aren't men peculiar?'

Her voice turned reflective. 'I wonder what birth-sign he is? I always like to know that about a man. It helps you cope, somehow.'

'He's a Leo.' The words came out without thinking, and Folly bit her lip. But fortunately Lisa didn't seem to notice that her new boss was surprisingly well informed about this particular customer.

'Is he? That's interesting. They're supposed to be good actors, aren't they? Well, you could have put that scene he made on at a theatre in the West End and charged for tickets, I reckon. And all about a few roses. I reckon he must be allergic to them or something.' She giggled. 'I suppose when you spend all that money on a girl you don't want to spend the evening wheezing into your hankie, do you? Especially not if she puts them by the bed.'

'Girl——?' Folly looked back at the list, but the names, in most cases just initial and surname, told her nothing. 'Don't be silly, Lisa. These will be business contacts, not personal friends.' At least in most cases, she thought. All except herself and Sexy Lexy. . .

Lisa looked at her as if she were suffering from softening of the brain. 'Go on,' she said scornfully. 'Why do you think all these businessmen have accounts anyway? So that they can send flowers to their girl-friends without their wives finding out.'

'But you don't actually know. . .?' Folly felt as if she were struggling against a tide. Some part of her still wanted to defend Luke Hunter, even though she was beginning to realise that he was far from being the man she thought she knew—the man she had let herself love. Her head felt swimmy; almost faint. 'I mean, they could be business contacts. With most of them there's nothing here to say what sex they are, even.'

'Not there, perhaps.' The other girl grinned. 'But he

likes to write the cards himself, doesn't he? So we've got them all stored up in Miss P's famous filing system. Of course, she keeps them locked—her precious "confidentiality"—but I know where she keeps the spare key.'

Folly's conflict of emotions must have shown on her face, because the other girl slapped a hand across her mouth. 'Oh, damn! I keep forgetting that you're not just another minion, like me.'

Lisa's frankness was quite beguiling, and, despite the fact that her world was tumbling down about her, Folly found herself liking her assistant more and more.

'You must think I'm awful. But honestly, Folly, I wouldn't dream of blackmailing them or whatever the old bat thinks I'm going to do. I just sneak a look, sometimes, when she's nipped out and I'm feeling a bit bored. It's better than television. Listen!'

She ducked down behind the table and emerged with the little box her employer had displayed so proudly, then raked around in the back of a drawer until she came up with a key. Folly watched in awful fascination as Lisa flicked through the cards. Somehow the last thing she wanted was concrete proof of Luke's betrayal, and yet here she was, actively searching for it. She felt as if an express train were speeding towards her—but her feet were set in concrete and there was nothing she could do.

'Listen to this one,' Lisa laughed in oblivious enjoyment. '"Sexy Lexy—you can still send shivers down my spine. Here's to the next five years." That's for next month—it must be their anniversary. I don't know who she is, but he thinks a lot of her. He's always sending her flowers—and last time I looked she was the only one on his list who got an "A". You know, lilies and orchids and all that—the top grade. She must live up to her name; most of the others are "C"s or less.'

She shuffled through the pack again. 'This lot are all "D"s. "Thank you for a wonderful week, Sandra." Or Helen, or Mary, or Carla—there's about ten of them, all with the same message. And all signed Luke. Honestly! The man's got a positive harem.'

The word had a sickeningly familiar sound. Folly wondered just how she could have been so naïve as to accept Luke's explanation of the porter's tale. 'But some of them must be business contacts, surely?' she said helplessly. If only Lisa would stop—but she had to know.

'Oh, yes—I suppose so. There's some boring ones as well.' Lisa gave an uninterested sniff. 'I mean, he must use the account for his business. But there's a lot that aren't. In fact, there was a new "A" just recently, I think—I remember old Philly saying something. She pretends to disapprove, but I think she's half in love with him herself.' She started to ferret through the cards again. 'What's the last name on that list?'

Folly cast her eye down the column of names, but it ran off the bottom of the page and she had to turn over. And when she came to the last name only the fact that she was already frozen saved her from betraying herself.

'I think that's enough, Lisa,' she said in a voice she hardly recognised. 'Those cards are private——'

But the other girl, engrossed in her search, didn't seem to hear her. 'Funny double-barrelled name it was—sounded foreign. Began with "T", I seem to remember—Tyler, or something.' Then inspiration struck. 'No—I remember, it was Taylor, because it was the same day you came in, and I remember thinking it was a coincidence. No—there doesn't seem to be a card here. Perhaps he's got sick of her already—I should think Luscious Luke is the love 'em and leave 'em type, wouldn't you?'

How could Lisa know him so well, when she herself had been so naïvely blind? Folly watched in agony, praying that now she had found no card she would lose interest. But the girl's fascination with this topic of gossip seemed unstoppable.

'What was that name, now?' She picked up the book. Folly wanted to snatch it away, but she could think of no good excuse. All she could do was hope that Lisa's sharp mind would fail to make the connection.

And at first it seemed she was lucky. 'Aphrosyne Taylor-Agathangelou, that was the one,' Lisa announced with satisfaction, but nothing else. 'Goodness, what a mouthful! But then, I was forgetting, you've got a foreign name too, haven't you? Or so Miss Philimore said.'

Lisa looked up, and although Folly swung away almost immediately it was too late. Their eyes had met—and she knew quite well what the other girl had read there.

They both sat there, not looking at each other, not daring to move. Lisa was the first to break the silence. 'Oh, lord,' she whispered. 'It was you, wasn't it? I *have* put my foot in it. Would you like me to crawl out quietly through the woodwork now or shall I wait and collect my cards?'

She sounded so apologetic that Folly almost laughed. But it met a lump of grief and anger at the back of her throat and came out more like a sob. Perhaps she ought to be grateful that, out of Luke Hunter's whole harem, she was at least one of the only two to be awarded an 'A'. But somehow she didn't feel grateful.

Sharing the honour with Sexy Lexy made it somehow even worse...

'Folly, are you all right? I'm sorry; I just didn't know... And all those things I said, I was just guessing really. I just gabble on—I didn't mean——'

'It's not your fault,' Folly managed through her sobs. 'You've done me a favour really. I'd rather know. At least—I did know, sort of, but I couldn't help hoping...'

'I know what you mean.' Lisa sounded as if she did. And Folly was suddenly swept with a wave of gratitude that it had been her assistant who had uncovered her secret, and not the pompous Miss Philimore. With a feeling of relief, she let go, and felt the tears run down her cheeks.

'That's better.' When her tears had run their course, Lisa handed her a final tissue and a mirror, and waited while she mopped herself dry. 'You needed that. But the question now is, what are you going to do?'

'Do? What to you mean? There isn't really anything to do; I just don't see him again. I've only known him a few weeks, after all.' She wished she felt as confident as she sounded. 'I'll get over it quickly enough.'

But her assistant shook her head in a gesture of impatience. 'That's not what I meant—of course you'll get *over* the rotten bastard. What I was wondering was how you were planning to get *even*.'

'Get *even*,' Folly repeated slowly. 'Revenge, you mean? I don't know. I hadn't thought of it—and anyway, what could I do?'

'Oh, I don't know. There must be heaps of things. Go to his office and make a scene, or send him some flowers there with a really embarrassing message, or something. If you say he's a Leo, you really want to try and puncture his dignity a bit. That'll get him.'

The idea had obviously caught Lisa's fancy. She grinned reminiscently. 'Once when a boyfriend did the dirty on me, I unpicked the seams of his best trousers and sewed them back together with tacking cotton. You know, that stuff that breaks easily? They split when he was in some really posh place, up the West End. Trying to impress his new girlfriend. I didn't half feel better after that. You can't just let him get away with it, Folly. You really can't.'

Folly felt the beginnings of a smile twitch her mouth. Lisa's story had conjured up an arresting image. And she had obviously been right to guess that her assistant possessed more initiative than her current employer gave her credit for.

'Honestly, Lisa, it's a nice thought. . .But if I made a scene I'm pretty sure it would be me who'd come out looking like a fool. He'd probably enjoy it—as you say, he's a dramatic sort of man. The flowers idea sounds better, but in all probability the only person to see them would be his secretary. And I bet he's got her well trained. So what's the point?'

'What's the point?' Lisa sounded quite indignant. 'The point is, to show him! To know that you've won! Look at you now—you're feeling miserable as hell, and I can't say I blame you. But wouldn't you feel a lot better if you knew that you'd kicked him back—and that he knew it too? Quite apart from the fact that if all the girls he'd ever dumped had had a go back he might have grown up to be less of a bastard.'

This time Folly's laughter didn't dissolve into tears. 'I suppose you could be right,' she admitted. It was certainly tempting. After all—hadn't one of the things that had made it so difficult to get over Tony been the fact that he'd got off scot-free? 'So what do I do?'

'"We", you mean. Two heads are better than one—and I feel I owe you on this. But it has to be something good, or it will just fizzle out like a damp squib and you'll feel worse than ever.'

Folly nodded. 'That's the trouble. Only you don't know him, Lisa—' She stopped, and started again. 'I mean—neither do I, obviously. Not really. Although I thought I did. . .But the one thing that does impress itself on you is that he's so very *competent*. I mean, it isn't going to be easy to make a fool of him.'

She watched Lisa's fingers shuffling aimlessly through the cards. 'And he doesn't care,' she added gloomily. 'With a harem like that to choose from, why should he care about losing one woman? He probably won't even notice I'm gone.'

'Then you'll have to make him notice. Can't you put sugar in his petrol tank or something? That should catch his attention.'

'And that of the police. He's already tried to have me arrested once—that's how we met, believe it or not.' Quickly Folly summed up the story of her meeting with Luke. Had it really been less than a month ago? It seemed like forever. . .

'Then what?' Lisa was obviously stronger on indignation than on practical ideas.

'I don't know. Something—appropriate, ideally.'

'What, like me posing as a beautiful heiress and getting him to fall madly in love with me, then dumping him?' Lisa struck a pose of melodramatic fervour and held it for a few seconds before slumping back in her seat. 'Nah—even if there *was* the slightest chance he'd fall for me, it wouldn't work. He'd just get one of the harem to comfort him.' She slapped the cards down on the table with an expression of disgust. 'It's a shame they don't know what he's like.'

Folly nodded again. Some of those other names might belong to women as naïve as she had been. 'Men like Luke Hunter ought to carry a government health warning,' she agreed. 'In fact, I'd like to tell them——'

She stopped, then started again excitedly. 'That's it! If they all knew what he was like, he'd have nowhere to run. Even a sheikh would be annoyed to lose the whole of his harem in one fell swoop.'

'So what would you do?' Lisa sounded doubtful. 'Go round to each in turn and announce yourself as the "other woman"? I don't want to pour cold water, Folly, but what if they didn't believe you? And think how embarrassing it would be. Besides,' she added practically, 'it might take weeks to catch them all in. Look what it's like when we're making deliveries. Half of them aren't in—and a message like that isn't something you can very well leave with a neighbour. Anyway, as soon as he found out what you were doing, he'd manage to stop you.'

But Folly's mind was working at top speed. 'Deliveries!' She almost shrieked the word. 'That's it! We'll say it with flowers—that way we can do it all in one night. And as for not believing me, they won't have much choice. Not when Luke's confessed in his own handwriting.'

'Forgery's against the law too, you know.'

But Folly ignored the other girl's sceptical expression. 'I don't mean forgery,' she crowed triumphantly. 'Oh, this is perfect, Lisa. Absolutely perfect. All we have to do is send some nice flowers to each of his girlfriends. Roses, I think, as he likes them so much. With one of his cards. Only. . .' She picked up the slips of pasteboard and let them fall haphazardly on the table in front of them. Then stirred them round with a finger.

She saw light dawn on the other girl's face, and nodded. 'Only I think they might get just a bit mixed up.'

CHAPTER EIGHT

'THANK goodness Miss Philimore's not here, or I'd have to explain this sudden run on roses.' Folly swept a mass of discarded foliage from the work-table to the bin. 'Now I can just go to Covent Garden Market tomorrow morning and replace what we've used. Much less strain on the imagination.'

Lisa nodded, carefully scooping up armful of bouquets to carry out to the van. 'Cheaper, as well. If you'd invented a string of lovelorn swains you'd have had to pay customer prices. This way, at least you'll get the local ones at trade. But the telephone orders are going to cost a fortune.'

Folly had been trying not to think about that particular angle of her revenge. 'I know,' she agreed reluctantly. 'And of course they won't be quite as effective because we can't use handwritten cards. But if we don't cover the full list the whole thing could fall flat. There's no point leaving him with half a harem, and there's no way of telling who's important and who's not.' Although she had an unpleasant feeling that she did know who formed the current centrepiece of this particular seraglio. That deep, sensual voice on the phone still rang in her ears.

'I suppose you're right.' The other girl laid the last of the flowers in position, and slammed the van doors shut. Then she hesitated, with the keys in her hand. 'I've mapped out a route to take you round, but are you sure you don't want me do the actual deliveries?

Or at least let me come with you and drive. The one-way systems round here can be pretty confusing.

For a moment Folly wavered. At the end of the street she could see the traffic building up. And for a number of reasons Lisa's moral support would have been welcome. But she shook her head. This was something between her, and Luke, and those other women he had betrayed. There was no room for an outsider. It was something she had to do alone.

'I want to have a look at them,' she said. It wasn't the full explanation, but it was true enough. She did want to see them; her rivals. Hunter's Harem. Especially Sexy Lexy, she added silently. The only other one of his women Luke Hunter had deemed worth an 'A'. . .

Stifling the pang of uncivilised jealousy that shot through her at that thought, Folly eased herself into the driver's seat and slammed the door. Then she edged the van gingerly out into the unfamiliar rush-hour traffic. As if to complete the gloomy atmosphere, it was beginning to rain.

Apart from the afternoon's normal deliveries, there were five names on Luke's list who lived within delivery distance of the Rose Bowl. One of them was 'Sexy Lexy'. Her address was less than a mile from the shop, but Folly had asked Lisa to keep it until last in the route she had mapped out. She hadn't formulated much of a plan, but she knew instinctively that if anything happened it would be there.

She glanced across at the dog-eared book of maps that lay on the passenger-seat beside her. She was almost at the first port of call—one of Luke's list. She realised suddenly that she was in the wrong lane, and pulled over sharply on the slippery road. Somewhere behind her a horn blared. But she hardly noticed it.

HUNTER'S HAREM   117

The address turned out to be a tiny basement flat at the bottom of a battered flight of steps. It hardly seemed a likely setting for the Wandas and Melissas of her imagination, and, for a moment, Folly was tempted to turn back. But then she remembered Tony, and how grateful she would have been to anyone who had had the courage to give her a hint of his real nature. . . Slowly she brought her finger up to the doorbell. And pressed it in.

The girl who answered was just that—hardly more than a girl. As she held out the flowers, and the bright young face lit up, Folly felt a fresh surge of anger against the man they held in common.

She hesitated on the edge of speech. Should she ask herself in; declare herself and deliver her warning in person? But the girl was already closing the door. And besides, she told herself as she hurried back to the van, it was kinder to do it impersonally.

This way they would be alerted to Luke's infidelity, but it wouldn't be forced on them. For those who were honest with themselves, the hint would be enough. And for those who weren't. . .well, no doubt Luke Hunter would turn up the charm and devise some plausible enough explanation. But the seed would have been planted. And perhaps they would never be fully at his mercy again.

The next two were out, and she had to leave the flowers with a neighbour. Then came a string of legitimate deliveries. Then another answer. This time the recipient was tall and blonde, with an air of glacier-like sophistication. Folly doubted if she would care what Luke got up to, but she gave her the flowers none the less. Then the woman smiled, and it changed her face completely.

'Dear Luke,' she said fondly, and, still standing on

the doorstep, plucked at the card. Folly turned tail and almost ran away.

There were a few more genuine orders to deliver. But Folly hardly noticed their faces, even though it was normally one of the highlights of the job to see other people's pleasure. Her mind was preoccupied with the last name on her list.

Soon she would see her—her rival. Soon she would know. . .But when she finally arrived at the little mews her heart gave a lurch. A large, black and dreadfully familiar BMW was parked outside.

'Luke. . .' She bit her lip, the significance of what she was seeing sinking home like a jagged knife between her ribs. He was with her, now, this minute. He might be touching her; holding her in his arms. . .Folly reached out uncertainly towards the ignition key, to kick the engine back into life and run away.

But something held her back. It suddenly seemed desperately important to meet the woman behind that haunting voice. Or at least to see her. She didn't want to think too closely about what she would do if Luke opened the door, but the driver had left an old anorak on the passenger-seat and she slipped it on, pulling the hood up to cover her hair. Then she jumped out of the van and went round to the back to unload.

Two Cellophane-wrapped sprays that she had been unable to deliver were lying on the bouquet of roses she had prepared for her rival. She swept them all up. She could hide her face behind them, if a disguise were needed. Though probably it wouldn't. Surely Sexy Lexy would answer her own front door?

It seemed forever before she heard footsteps coming towards the door. But as the door swung open Folly found herself wishing that it had stayed firmly shut.

Luke Hunter was standing only feet away from her, almost filling the door with his towering presence.

She stared at him from behind the barrier of her flowers, wordlessly holding out the paper-wrapped roses. She couldn't have spoken if she had tried. Her eyes were on a level with his chest, where his tie hung crookedly from a casually loosened knot. And, when she looked up, was it just her imagination? Or did that gold-brown mane of hair look more than usually rumpled? As if he had been disturbed. . .

Folly was bitterly certain that she could guess at what.

He bent forward to take the bouquet, and she felt something inside her tighten and twist as she shrank further behind her flowers. But Luke showed no signs of noticing her. How could he be so close, and not know she was there? Her own awareness of him was so strong that she felt she could have tracked him anywhere, just by the dizzying sensation of his presence.

Then he smiled, and thanked her in that tearingly familiar voice, and suddenly she could hardly bear to think that she had lost him. She wanted to speak to him, to shout, to scream, to plead. . .

But before she could open her mouth another familiar voice came floating from the house behind him. 'What is it, Luke?' Somewhere above, Folly heard footsteps, and she started edging towards the van. She had wanted to see her rival—but she had reckoned without the effect Luke would have on her senses. To see them together would be more painful than she could bear.

Then Luke spoke again, raising his voice to address the woman behind the scenes. 'Go back to bed, Lexy. It's just some flowers—I'll bring them up.'

That finished it. Folly turned her back and almost ran the last steps to the sanctuary of the waiting van. She dumped the bouquets she was still carrying on to the passenger-seat. Then, hardly knowing what she was doing, she drove wildly away.

The telephone was already ringing by the time Folly returned to the flat, and she had almost picked it up before realising that the only person likely to be ringing her was Luke. And that he was the one person in the world she definitely did not want to speak to.

Besides, there was something else she had to do. Wrenching the phone line once more from its socket, she walked mechanically through to the bedroom and pulled open the drawer of the desk. A small pile of cards lay before her, now horribly familiar. The latest on top.

So many cards. And she had been in London for less than a month. It hadn't taken long to make a fool of herself. 'Thank you for a wonderful evening. . .'

But her emotions had burnt themselves out, and all she felt as she picked up the cards and carried them through to the kitchen was a dull emptiness, as if the pain she wasn't feeling had left a gap. And a feeling of waste. She had thought there was something special between them. She had felt it. 'A wonderful evening. . .' But it had all been a sham.

Dry-eyed, Folly walked over to the sink and turned on the tap. Then the waste disposal machine.

Such a waste. She fed the little slips of cardboard one by one into its grinding jaws. Then she went back through the flat and collected the vases. One by one, the blooms Luke Hunter had sent her so unthinkingly were reduced to a green herbal mulch and flushed down the drain. Then she set to with bleach and scouring pads to render the vases spotless.

Only when that was done, and she had put them away out of sight, did she begin to wonder what her next move would be. Her first thought was that she would have to leave the flat. Now; at once. She would have to go back to the hotel, or find another just as bad, and resume the soul-destroying trudge from one unsuitable rabbit-hutch to another.

She had got as far as pulling out her suitcase, which looked scruffier than ever now that her eyes had accustomed themselves to the comfortable luxury of Luke Hunter's flat, and laying it open on the bed before something inside her rebelled.

'No,' she said aloud, slamming the case shut and thrusting it back into oblivion. 'Why should I? He said "No strings", after all. I'll stay until I've found somewhere decent. And if he wants to get rid of me he'll have to throw me out.'

Then she glanced at her watch and saw to her amazement that it was already midnight. If she was to replace the roses she had used, she realised wearily, she would need to be up again at four. She wandered through to the kitchen to get her bag, and checked through her notes for the name and address of the Rose Bowl's usual wholesaler. The thought of leaving was already drifting out of her mind.

A little voice inside her whispered that Luke had never intended his generous words to be taken literally. It had been a convenient fiction to smooth the path towards what he must have seen as their inevitable destiny in that great, soft bed. After all, why should he have expected her to hold out when so many others had succumbed?

And, now she'd burnt her boats so very finally, he

would want it back. Ready for the next applicant to his harem. If she stayed, he would be furious.

But Folly realised that she didn't care.

'Is there a problem? I've been waiting half an hour. All I wanted was a few roses, for goodness' sake.' Folly couldn't understand what was taking the man so long. All around her, the flower-market was bustling with life as traders seemingly managed to clinch three deals simultaneously, talking and haggling at double speed. But in her small corner it was as if time had decided to take an extended coffee-break.

The wholesaler looked embarrassed. 'Er—Jim's just got to OK it with the boss,' he said uncertainly. 'Because you're new, like. He won't be long.' Folly felt instinctively that he was lying; but why, she couldn't imagine. And there was nothing she could do. Except wait.

She shifted from foot to foot and stared up impatiently at the gallery of offices that ran around the walls. There was no sign of the absent Jim. Other customers arrived, made their purchases and left. Money changed hands, flickering from one to another with almost invisible speed. Porters pushed past, their trolleys piled high with sweet-smelling burdens.

And still no one came. Folly found herself reading the labels on boxes stacked around her. The names and the places. Gerbera; gypsophila; gladioli and freesia. Amsterdam, Cornwall, and Spain. The scent of moist earth and crushed stems filled her nostrils, driving the last traces of sleep from her early-morning brain.

At any other time, the sights, sounds and smells of the covered market would have delighted her. But now she felt cocooned in her own private shell of misery, as

HUNTER'S HAREM

cut off from the noise and activity around her as if she were frozen in ice.

Alstroemeria; aquilegia——but the sound of footsteps behind her penetrated her numbness, and she swung round. Surely this must be the elusive Jim at last? But the figure that stood before her was the last she had expected to see.

'Luke!'

She shrank back against the pile of boxes. But when he spoke the anger she had expected was under tight control.

'Restocking on roses, are you, Folly? I think we need to talk.' The curt words were almost more frightening than the expected explosion would have been.

She tried to shake her head, but found she was pressed so hard against the stack behind her that movement was impossible. Or was it just fear that paralysed her, like a frightened rabbit? 'Luke, I——'

But the sound of her own craven voice seemed to wake the ghosts of resistance that were slumbering inside her. 'I don't see what we have to talk about,' she said more strongly. 'I told you before; I'm not interested in joining your harem. There must be plenty of other women in the world. So why pick on me?'

There; that was it. Now she would see his eyes flash dark with anger, and hear his voice crack. . .But he only smiled one of those predatory smiles that she was coming to dread. 'I'm not sure,' he admitted, with an air of confession. Although anything less repentant than the way he was looking at her now, Folly thought, would be hard to imagine. More than ever, he was the hunter. And she was his prey.

He leaned a hand casually against the wall of boxes, closing the trap still further. 'I think it must be your eyes,' he said at last, running his own gaze up and down as if giving intimate consideration to every other feature of her body. Folly felt nakedly vulnerable, and, to her shame, a thrill of excitement ran through her before she could suppress it.

'Don't bother, Luke.' The market was a public place, after all. If she stood firm, there was nothing he could do, she told herself—though whether she believed it was another matter. 'There's no point thinking you can flatter your way out of this. I may be rather naïve for the big city, but I'm learning fast. And I'm not going to listen to any more of your lies.'

But he carried on as if she hadn't spoken. 'Yes, I think it must be your eyes. Either that, or I've got a secret penchant for women who attack me with briefcases and then do their best to alienate half my workforce.'

His free hand came up to touch her lightly on the cheek. Folly tried to flinch away, but he was so close that every movement seemed to bring him closer. His voice purred compellingly on. 'But, on balance, I think it's the eyes. There's something about them that makes me want to see them glazed with passion——'

She felt herself flush deep red to her hair. 'Oh, do shut up about my eyes!' Then something occurred to her. 'And how did you know it was me who sent the flowers anyway? And how did you find me here?'

If Luke had shrugged his shoulders and claimed a diabolic omniscience she would have been disposed to believe him. But he just raised his eyebrows, looking down at her with mocking disdain. 'I saw you, of course. I admit I might not have paid much attention to an anonymous delivery girl, but they don't normally bolt when they see me, which attracted my attention. That disgusting hood you were wearing slipped, and I got a good look at the back of your head. At first I assumed that Lexy's flowers were just an aberration of your filing system. But when I got home and found my answerphone knee-deep in angry messages I didn't really have to be Sherlock Holmes to work out that you had something to do with it.'

When he got home... Despite her situation, Folly felt a illogical sense of relief that he hadn't spent the night in Lexy's bed. She must have thrown him out. Folly found herself smiling. Perhaps her plan had accomplished its objective after all.

She blinked to find Luke glaring down at her. 'I'm so glad you find the situation funny,' he said sarcastically. 'And as to how I found you—when you didn't answer the phone I went round to the flat. And found your notebook on the kitchen table, conveniently open at the name of this place. I made a quick phone call to make sure you didn't leave before I got here, and then came straight round. I hope I didn't keep you waiting too long?'

So he'd been looking for her. If she had been there...'*My* flat, Luke, at the moment. You had no right——'

'I had every right. You were my guest, remember? And, since all the evidence pointed to your having gone completely berserk, I thought it my duty as your host to ask one or two questions. Like, what the hell did you think you were doing last night? And why?'

She stared back at him uncomfortably, her mind turning over possible avenues of escape. 'You mean the flowers?'

'I mean the flowers, yes. I mean the wholesale alienation of my entire sales staff. Little things like that.'

So that was the line he was planning to take. 'Don't make me laugh, Luke. I saw the list, remember? And the cards. And the women, come to that. If they were all your sales staff, I'll eat a copy of the Sex Discrimination Act.'

'I'll bear that in mind. But for the moment, why not humour me with a little explanation?'

'I don't see why I should.' Folly's face was pink with defiance. 'You didn't bother to explain that you were breaking our date on Thursday night.'

For a moment, she seemed to have wrong-footed him. 'What's that supposed to mean?' he demanded. 'I mean, I'm sorry I couldn't get through to you on Thursday evening, but I did try, and got cut off. And then either you weren't answering or there was something wrong with the phone. But after all, you already knew there was a problem——'

'I knew nothing!' The anger and hurt she had felt gathered together in one anguished cry. 'Why didn't you contact me, Luke? Surely, however busy you were, you could have got a message through? I was sitting there all dressed up, waiting.' Her voice began to peter out as the tears threatened. 'I even bought a new dress. . .'

Luke's anger seemed temporarily in abeyance. 'But of course you knew,' he said in obvious puzzlement. 'On Thursday morning, when I realised I was going to have to go away urgently on business, I came into the shop to try and find you. But you weren't there, so I left a message with your Miss Philimore. Are you telling me the old bat didn't pass it on?'

Folly felt her mouth fall slowly open. 'Oh. . .But she was ill, Luke. She came down with this summer flu everyone's getting and went home before I got in. She must have forgotten. . .'

Luke didn't seem inclined to accept a dose of flu as sufficient excuse. 'Stupid old fool,' he muttered wrathfully. 'You mean to tell me that's what started this whole fiasco off? Because you thought I'd stood you up?'

But Folly stood her ground. Even if his explanation was true, it didn't excuse the other counts against him. 'No, Luke—it wasn't just that. I told you—I just didn't fancy being another name on your list. And I particularly didn't like you getting another member of your harem to phone me up on Thursday night and make your excuses. For your information, before that phone call was cut off, I heard quite enough to know it wasn't you who made it.'

Luke was still staring at her as if she had gone mad. 'You're not making any sense, Folly. If we're talking about the same phone call, the reason it was a woman who spoke to you was that we were both travelling in my car at the time—and I was driving. So she dialled, and she was about to pass it across to me when the line went dead. Are you telling me you've built some jealous fantasy out of two seconds on the phone? I told you before—the only harem I have is a working one. And if you don't damn well believe me——'

It sounded so convincing—but then, according to Lisa, Leos were known for their acting abilities. And, for once, she had the upper hand. 'Oh, why bother, Luke?' she broke in angrily. 'I've seen the list, remember? The account list at the Rose Bowl, with my name on it. Along with all the others. I suppose I should be flattered that you gave me an "A"—though I'd be better pleased if you thought enough of me to send my flowers in person, instead of by remote control. At least that way I wouldn't have got a note thanking me for a "wonderful evening" that never happened.'

She laughed bitterly. 'That's when I thought a little research might be in order. And it was really most instructive. Not only did I discover that all these tender little messages you keep sending me were probably written weeks in advance, but I also discovered just how many other women I share that privilege with. Fifteen, was it? Or twenty? I really can't remember. But I really do find it difficult to believe that they are all "business contacts". Unless your business is something rather more old-fashioned than sales and marketing.'

She could almost see the thought processes flicker across his brain. 'Damn the woman! I told her to cancel those flowers.' Luke swung away, punching at a box of tulips with one furious hand. Then he turned back towards her. 'I set your name up on the account the first time we met. I wanted to see you again, but I was dashing all over Europe that week, and I didn't have time to chase you in person, so I thought I'd say it with flowers. But since then I've never used it—up until this week. And then it was only because I knew I was going to have to leave at the crack of dawn on Friday, and I wouldn't have time to fix anything up.'

'So you just dreamt up a message? You must find our evenings together remarkably predictable.'

Luke's eyes flashed angrily at her sneering tone, but he made an evident effort to control himself. 'I can see how you might think it was insincere, but that wasn't how it seemed to me at the time. I just wanted you to know I was thinking of you. Is that such a crime? And when I found out my Friday meeting was being moved forward and I wouldn't be seeing you after all I asked your Miss Philimore to cancel it. But she seems to have quite a talent for forgetting my instructions.'

'She does, doesn't she?' Despite herself, Folly found herself wondering if Luke's tale could be true, and the oversights made with deliberate spite. He was so dangerously persuasive—and it would be all too convenient to blame everything on the absent Miss Philimore.

But what she had to remember was that, however convincing he might sound on details, there was a hard core of fact that even Luke Hunter could never explain away. She had been there, at Lexy's house, and she had seen him. . . And she had seen those other women too. And nothing he could say would make her forget them.

Summoning her courage, she pushed past him into the gangway between the stalls, then leapt aside as a porter nearly ran her over with a loaded trolley. Luke dragged her back, the tips of his fingers burning on her arm like lighted coals.

'What the hell's the matter with you, Folly? OK, so I ordered some flowers in advance. And a female colleague dialled your number from my car. Is that the sum total of the charges against me? Is that what sparked all this off?'

What did the man expect, for goodness' sake? That with one word from him she would behave as if nothing had happened? 'Why should I believe a word you say, Luke? What do you want from me?'

She regretted asking the question as soon as the words were out. Luke's eyes licked over her in a way that made his answer perfectly clear. 'No, why should you?' he echoed, with a sort of bitter mockery. 'Why should you trust me at all? And as for what I want from you, I hardly think this is the time or place to tell you that. Though it does figure in my plans. But right now, all I want is a fair hearing. And it seems I won't get it until you've had a chance to simmer down. What I'd suggest is a relaxing weekend in the country. So how does that sound?'

'A *what*?' Folly stared at him open-mouthed. Was he really so unbelievably sure of his charms that he thought he had only to indicate his wishes for them to be fulfilled? 'You must be joking. I wouldn't spend the weekend with you if——'

'How about *if* it was the only way you could save yourself losing every corporate customer you've got?' There was a long pause. 'Yes, I thought that might catch your attention. Think about it, Folly. How many of your business accounts would stay if they knew what sort of "discretion" you were offering?' His smile belied the cruelty of his words. But Folly knew which to believe.

'You wouldn't. . .' But she knew he would. Why should he hesitate to crush her? Her attempt at revenge had gone wildly, dangerously wrong. And all she had achieved was to plunge herself still deeper in his power.

CHAPTER NINE

FOLLY couldn't believe that she was letting this happen. Why hadn't she stood her ground; simply called Luke's bluff—even pleaded with him if she'd thought it would do any good? But instead, she had let him drive her back to the flat; had stood by in mute acquiescence while he'd ransacked her drawers and cupboards and packed her a bag.

And now here she was, sitting meekly in the passenger-seat of his car, while he drove her out of London with the controlled aggression of a racing driver. An angry racing driver. Folly tried to sink back inconspicuously into the soft leather seat and take stock.

The results were unpromising. She was being carried at considerably over the legal speed-limit towards an unknown destination—and quite possibly what a Victorian heroine would have regarded as a 'fate worse than death', since she could hardly imagine that Luke had gone to the trouble of virtually kidnapping her in order to spend a quiet weekend playing Scrabble.

It was one result of her 'revenge' that both she and Lisa had failed to predict. But since she had wrecked Luke's plans for a country weekend with Lexy, and deprived him of the possibility of replacing her from the ranks of his unofficial harem, perhaps it was hardly surprising that he should demand that she herself should fill the gap. Willingly or not.

Not that Luke Hunter would ever descend to anything as crude as rape. Folly was quite surprised to find she had no fears on that score. His Leo pride, if nothing else, would demand her willing consent. But, with a sinking feeling that chilled her more than any explosion of anger on his part, she realised that she was far from sure that such consent would be denied.

It was shameful, almost unbelievable, but she still wanted him. What else could explain her presence now, in his car? He had accosted her in a public place, and yet she hadn't screamed, or run, or asked for help. And even now the closeness of him was acting like a drug on her tired senses, its effect heightened by a heady mixture of desire and fear.

Once they were alone together, once he touched her, she would be lost. Whether or not she believed his excuses, her own body, her own impulsive longings, would betray her. Her only hope lay in escape. Folly stared blankly out at the speeding countryside and tried to work out what her strategy should be.

But twenty minutes later, as the big car swung off the motorway and began to thread its way along country roads, her mind was still a blank. If a swirling spiral of panic could be called a blank. Neither of them had spoken a word since leaving London. Then suddenly Luke spoke.

'We're almost there,' he said shortly. The car turned into a narrow lane. And then, before she could prepare herself, Luke swung them through a wide gateway buried deeply in the trees.

'This is it.'

She almost held her breath. But the vista that opened before them was so fantastic that for a few moments she almost forgot to be afraid. The mellow stone of the edifice—she hesitated to call it a house—was modelled into an elaborate copy of a French château, complete with round, steepled towers at the corners and an intricate garden laid out in the foreground. . .

There was even, she realised with a sense of unreality, a fountain playing in the pool at the centre of the design. And could that bird that Luke had just swerved to avoid really have been a *peacock*?

'Luke, what is this place?' she said faintly. 'Is it a hotel?' She was jerked forward as he slammed on the brakes and brought the car skidding to a halt on the gravel in front of the steps.

'Never mind that now. I'll explain it later.' He was already opening the door to climb out. 'All this has delayed me. If we hurry, we'll just be on time.'

'On time for what——?' But Luke was already climbing the stone steps up to the arched front door, and Folly's question went unheard. Forgetting her half-formed resolution to stay in the car, she scrambled out on to the gravel path and started to follow him up the steps.

'Luke, thank goodness you're here.' Folly's eyes jerked upwards at the hoarse whisper to see her escort being greeted by a plumpish middle-aged woman with steel-grey hair and a worried expression. 'I don't feel quite so bad this morning, but my voice has gone completely. And three of the girls have gone down with it too. You'll have to go straight on in. I don't know what I'd have done if you'd been any later—the girls are getting terribly impatient.'

Then Folly reached the top of the steps, and the woman noticed her for the first time. 'Who's this, then?' she croaked. 'The latest addition to your harem?' But, although she smiled briefly at Folly in a friendly enough way, she seemed too distracted to wait for an answer, and started to usher them inside.

Which was just as well, thought Folly, as she would hardly have known how to reply. What had the woman meant about 'the girls'—surely Luke hadn't brought more than one of his conquests here together? And what sort of woman was she anyway, to treat his Casanova habits with such casual indifference? Folly shivered. There was something sinister about that murmuring voice...

Then another urgent whisper broke in on her thoughts. 'The girls are waiting in the Seraglio, so if I take...' She paused for Folly to supply her name. 'If I take Folly here through to get undressed, you could go in and get the others warmed up.'

To her horror, Folly saw Luke nod and turn away down the corridor, leaving her alone with this sinister whispering woman who seemed to take it for granted that she was meekly going to strip off and join in what could only be some kind of orgy. In a seraglio! It was impossible—things like that didn't happen in England. Not the England her mother had described. And yet...

She clutched her jacket defensively against her breasts. 'That won't be necessary,' she said in as firm a voice as she could manage. 'I'm quite comfortable like this.'

The older woman looked at her doubtfully. 'You'll feel rather overdressed,' she whispered painfully. 'And you'll want to take your things off eventually, won't you? Or what are you here for? But I suppose if you don't want to miss the start you could just go straight in.'

Folly tried to protest that she didn't want to go *in* at all, but her guide's businesslike attitude and obvious haste made it difficult to intervene. And paradoxically, now Luke had gone, she felt more alone and more afraid than ever. It was as if he had been her protector, instead of the very opposite...

And besides, there was a robust corner of her mind

that refused to believe what was happening. This was England, after all. England was a civilised country, where policemen were happy to tell you the time and give you directions in the street. Things like this just didn't happen. And if she spoke up and then it turned out to be a mistake. . . Reduced to speechlessness by the conflicting emotions that tore at her, she found herself meekly following where her whispering 'captor' led.

This turned out to be a pair of double doors at the end of a corridor. 'The Seraglio complex is through there,' her guide croaked, with as little drama as if she had been showing the way to the bathroom. 'The changing-room is on the right, when you want to undress. And now if you'll excuse me, I really must go to bed and nurse this throat before I lose my voice altogether. Enjoy yourself—you'll find Mr Hunter always makes these sessions as pleasant as possible for all concerned.'

Almost without knowing how she had got there, Folly found herself on the other side of the double doors, pushing through a curtain of leaves that shrouded the entrance. And staring at a scene that, at first sight, made the annals of ancient Rome look like a Sunday School picnic. . .

It was like something out of a film set—and not the sort of film that was recommended for family viewing. The general effect was of a tropical jungle, made somehow rich and sinfully luxurious. All around the walls of the circular seraglio, potted palms and other plants tangled together in profusion, almost concealing the carved archways and marble columns that led the eye upwards to the intricately decorated ceiling. Even the atmosphere was tropical, its moist, warm heaviness making Folly's clothes cling uncomfortably to her skin.

Vapour from a heated pool in the centre of the floor obscured Folly's vision with a steamy, exotically scented mist, but, even so, she could see that she was not alone. Low couches and upholstered cushions were dotted around the floor. And on them, talking and laughing, sat so many women that Folly closed her eyes in shock. Surely not even Luke Hunter. . .

But the women were still there when she looked again; twenty or thirty of them, in various states of undress—although none, she was relieved to notice once she could take things in, was actually naked. Most wore bikinis or swimsuits; a few were swathed in towels. One girl of about nineteen was wrapped in a brightly coloured sarong and Folly recognised her with a shock as one of the women to whom she had delivered the flowers.

The memory seemed to bring the scene back into focus. So it was true, then. This was Hunter's harem. And she had been fool enough to let him draw her in to it.

Folly shrank backwards towards the heavy curtain of vegetation behind her—whether to escape or merely hide she wasn't quite sure. But then her movement was arrested by the sound of a door opening and closing on the far side of the room, and a voice that she recognised only too well.

An expectant silence fell over the room and Folly watched, mesmerised, as Luke Hunter stepped forward on to a small raised dais at one side of the pool. To her relief, he was still fully dressed, although he had taken off his jacket as a concession to the almost tropical heat. She could see the sweat beading on his forehead.

And through the pain that twisted inside her she could still feel his physical attraction like a magnetic force—and she knew that every other woman in the room could feel it too. The atmosphere was suddenly charged with a dangerous sexual electricity.

'Good morning, ladies.' There was a chorus of murmured greeting in response. 'I'm sorry to keep you waiting,' he went on, 'but those of you who have been here before will know that I like to say a few words to break the ice before we get down to the real business of the weekend. Which is——' his voice deepened to a husky growl '—pleasure. Sheer pleasure, with a capital "P". Not just the lazy pleasure of the Seraglio, although I hope you'll enjoy the pools, the sauna and the massage facilities. Nor just the pleasures of the table, although I can promise you that the chef here is superb. But I hope you will also enjoy the other activities we'll be exploring later today, and tomorrow—collectively and individually.'

Folly could imagine what sort of 'activities' he meant, although the thought of such collective revelry made her mind twist away from the image it evoked. But his speech seemed a curiously formal introduction to what she supposed was some kind of orgy. Nor did the other women seem to be responding quite as she expected.

But there was no time to think it out. Luke was speaking again—and this time the eyes were turning in her own direction.

'. . .and this is Folly, who will be joining us for the first time this weekend. She looks a little hot and flustered at the moment, which I'm afraid is my fault for rushing her down here at very little notice. But I'm sure that once she joins you in the pool she will find it easy enough to slip into the flow of things. Folly, why don't you go and undress now, and join the others back here?'

His eyes rested on her, mocking her, and Folly knew

that it was now or never. She had to stand up to him; shout out that she wouldn't let herself become embroiled in his sordid games. . . She ought to demand to be taken back to London. Now; immediately.

But the words wouldn't come. Instead, she felt herself flush deep red as she started to withdraw, trying to calculate her chances if she made a run for the exit instead of the changing room. The two doors were next to each other—would he notice if she took the wrong one? And if he did, would he pursue her?

Her hand was on the handle. Luke had turned his attention back to the other women, and none of them had attention to spare for anyone but him. It was worth a try. . .

'And now, on to the first part of our programme.' The very ordinariness of Luke's tone caught Folly's attention and she paused, her muscles still tensed to run. 'I want to introduce the man who has made this all possible, and whose health and leisure complex you are here to experience—and later, of course, to promote. I'm sure that after this weekend you will have no problem in breaking all Lucas Sales's previous records on this contract. And if any extra incentive were needed, apart from that of selling a superlative product, you'll be pleased to hear that our client intends to offer monthly awards—in the shape of all-inclusive weekend passes to the Seraglio.'

There was a murmur of appreciation from the assembled women. Folly just stared, her mind spinning as she tried to fit these new facts into perspective. She hardly noticed as Luke's place on the dais was taken by a small, fat man who was looking very warm and uncomfortable in his business suit. Unlike Luke, he had unwisely decided to retain his jacket, presumably in the interests of looking businesslike, and was obviously regretting his decision. Vaguely she heard him talking of 'luxury leisure complexes' and 'total pleasure environments'. But the world didn't begin to make sense again until Luke Hunter returned to the stand.

'And now, ladies, I'll just run through the programme for the weekend. This morning is free for you to enjoy the Seraglio and discover its selling points for yourselves. Then after lunch I will be giving the first of our seminars on marketing and salesmanship, with particular reference to leisure services and luxury products, to be followed by a discussion and work in groups.' He paused. 'Unfortunately, our sales manager, Mrs Everard, has contracted this flu bug that's going round, so you'll have to put up with me all today—and possibly tomorrow too, if she doesn't regain her voice.'

The murmur of amusement that ran round the gathering made it obvious that none of the women present saw this as a hardship. 'It's a full programme and, I hope, a very enjoyable one. So I'll just say thank you to the management of the Seraglio for allowing this conference to take place in such pleasant surroundings, and to you ladies for giving up your weekend to be here. And now I'll leave you to enjoy yourselves. Have a good time—and I'll see you at lunch.'

Luke stepped backwards off the dais, then strode swiftly from the room, with the little man bobbing like a cork in his wake. For a few seconds after their departure, the room was silent. Then one of the women nearest the pool let her towel fall down by her feet.

'Well, here goes nothing,' she said cheerfully, and jumped in.

The movement broke the spell, and a hubbub of

laughter and shouting replaced the silence as one woman after another jumped gleefully into the pool.

And Folly let her hand unclench from its grip on the door-knob, and let the exit door fall shut. Praying, as she sidled along to the changing-room, that no one would ever know how utterly wrong she had been. . .

'For a moment there, I thought you were going to run.' As Folly exited from the changing-rooms, the sound came from behind her, and she swung round to see Luke leaning against the wall, looking across at the scenes of relaxation in the Seraglio with a look of malicious amusement on his face. 'But I see you're still with us. Does that mean you plan to join in the fun?'

Folly clutched the towel closer around her, painfully aware that the bikini he had packed for her was the briefest she owned. 'Yes, of course.' Whatever happened, she must never let him find out just how close to running she had really been. 'I thought I'd start with a dip in the hot tub. But it looks a bit full, so I might try the sauna instead.' And indeed, the bubbling waters of the hot pool in the centre of the room seemed full of shrieking women.

But Luke shook his head. 'The sauna's pretty crowded too, I would think. I just saw three of the girls go in. But if you want to try a hot tub I can do better than that. I've got the VIP suite here—and there's a private jacuzzi attached which you're welcome to try.'

He looked at her questioningly as she hesitated. 'And it would give us a chance to talk, Folly,' he added softly. 'In private. That may not be easy this weekend.'

'All right, then.' Folly threw caution to the winds. After all, she did owe Luke something after the stupid way she had behaved. And, although she was rapidly coming to the conclusion that she had made a fool of herself all down the line, she still didn't quite know *how*. Or why. . .He was right, they had a lot to talk about. And perhaps now was the time.

Feeling rather conspicuous in her towel and bikini, she followed him up to the palatially decorated VIP suite, and into the bathroom—trying not to notice the bedroom they passed through on the way. Fortunately, it was obvious that Luke had done no more than drop off a suitcase. Even the great wide bed had an impersonal air. . .Otherwise it might have been a great deal more difficult to ignore.

Off the bathroom was another smaller room which contained the jacuzzi. Luke waved her ahead. 'You go in—I'll be with you in a moment. I just want to take a shower.'

At least that meant she wouldn't have to discard her towel under Luke's assessing gaze, Folly thought. For the first time, she started to relax and take in her surroundings. Beside the low built-in tub was a control panel with a number of dials and, by a process of experimentation, she managed to transform the still pool into a seething cauldron of bubbles.

It looked quite terrifying—but somehow enticing at the same time. Like Luke himself, perhaps. And then she heard a movement in the next room, and, dropping her towel hastily on the floor by the tub, she slipped gingerly into the steaming water. It was even hotter than she expected, and she gave an involuntary yelp.

'It's too hot,' Luke said unnecessarily as he came through, towelling water from his tangled hair. Wet, it looked darker—a deep bronze rather than gold. He wore nothing but a towel and although she tried to keep her eyes upon his chest a line of damp, curling hair drew them inexorably downwards. Down past his navel, to where the towel's bleached whiteness stretched taut across his hips. . .

And then, somehow, the towel had been discarded. And he was in the jacuzzi with her, turning up the dials until the water bubbled furiously around them. Folly held herself stiff, hardly daring to move.

'So—I gather you didn't fancy joining my "harem"?' Luke's teasing threw a new light on the situation, and Folly forgot her nervousness as she turned to him in indignation, spluttering as the sudden movement sent a wave of bubbling water splashing across her face.

'You mean you knew?' she gasped. 'You knew what I was thinking? And you did it on purpose?'

But he only grinned, and stretched his legs out luxuriantly, leaning back on the narrow underwater bench that circled the edge of the pool and extending one casual arm behind her head.

She could feel the almost-accidental brush of his hand against her hair and felt herself flood with a warmth deeper and more insistent than the scalding heat of the water in which they were immersed. It was a position of strange intimacy; as if the steam that shrouded them was a veil that cut out the world.

She left her head where it was, and glimpsed the satisfaction that flew across Luke's face. So he hadn't been sure of her after all. . .

His fingers caressed her again, more blatantly this time. 'I told you from the start that my relationship with my "harem" was purely a business one. It was hardly my fault if you chose to misinterpret it.' An aggrieved note entered his voice. 'And do you realise you nearly wrecked this conference for me? After I'd spent the last two days setting it up?'

'Me?' Folly's face was too pink with the heat to blush

any more, but it felt as if it was trying. 'What do you mean?' But she had a terrible feeling she knew.

Fortunately, Luke's anger seemed to have evaporated along with the steam that surrounded them. 'I mean that, when the client suggested giving our sales force a taste of the product they were selling, I had to put it all together at ultra-short notice—and the only way I managed to get my people to drop everything and come was by stressing how much I relied on each of them individually. Finding out that I apparently couldn't even remember their names in the right order rather spoilt the effect. I had to do a lot of talking to get out of that one, Folly. So I thought you deserved a bit of a fright in return.'

'You certainly gave me that.' Even though it was beginning to recede in her memory, Folly still couldn't quite see what she had gone through as a joke. 'And I think you're being a bit unfair, Luke. All the evidence seemed to point. . .' Folly's voice petered out as some of her doubts started to reassert themselves. 'I mean, bosses don't usually send flowers to their employees, do they? Not with messages like that.' The doubt was joined by a faint tone of shrewish suspicion. 'And for that matter, not many men are lucky enough to have a work-force composed entirely of beautiful women.'

He laughed out loud, and she could feel the vibrations through the water. Or no—not through the water. Somehow, he had moved closer, and their thighs were pressed together on the wooden seat. And if she turned towards him, her left breast would brush against his chest. . .

'This isn't my entire work-force, my little idiot.' His voice seemed to fill the few inches' space between them, bringing them even closer. She could feel his breath on her cheek. 'Just a very important section of it. But this place—the Seraglio—is a luxury health club for *women*. It made sense to me and the client to have women selling it. After all, this way they can extol its benefits woman-to-woman; and that's why the client wanted them to experience it for themselves.'

An almost irresistible magnetism was pulling her round to face him, eye to eye. Or mouth to mouth. . .Folly struggled against it, clutching at the thread of normality his explanation offered and resolutely keeping her face towards the centre of the tub. 'Oh.' It was so obvious when he explained it. 'You mean, you employ men as well?'

'Of course I do, my little idiot. Lunch today will include a copy of the Sex Discrimination Act, *à la crème*.' He grinned. 'Although, in fact, a lot of my top sales people are women; especially on the telephone-selling side. The voice is very important then, and people usually find a female voice more persuasive than a man's.'

'But. . .' Folly was losing track now of which arguments he had demolished. 'But what about the flowers? Surely you don't send them to your male employees as well?' She had the feeling that he knew very well what a struggle was going on beneath her words—and that he was amused by it. But he seemed happy to play along—like a cat with a mouse. Or a lion. . . Did lions toy with their prey?

'Why not? Most people like flowers around the house.' He grinned, and relented a little. 'Although, I agree, some of them might not think it very appropriate. But then, some women don't, either. There are a variety of little tokens I can use when I want to say "thank you" for some special effort—chocolates, gift tokens and so on, as well as flowers. I just use whichever the person in question prefers.'

It no longer occurred to Folly to doubt that Luke was telling the truth—and she knew that she was concentrating on his explanation simply as a shield againt the other questions that hovered only a breath away. But somehow she couldn't let go. 'I still think it's a bit odd that not only are your staff here all women, but also all stunningly attractive to boot. That hardly sounds like a "necessary qualification" for telephone sales. Are you sure you don't recruit them with a casting couch?'

But Luke just laughed. She felt the puff of his breath on her ear, and it took all the determination she possessed not to turn round. His lips must be so close. . .'I think there are at least three misconceptions in that speech,' he murmured gently, his words stirring the soft down of her cheek. Surely he must be almost touching her now? But she didn't dare look.

'What do you mean?'

'For a start, it's my sales manager who does the recruiting—and she's a woman as well. Very sexist of you to assume otherwise, if I may say so. And, before your mind starts wandering off into even more lurid byways, she's extremely happily married, with three grown-up children. And she's the wrong side of fifty. In fact, you met her on your way in.'

'Oh.' Folly took that in, while trying to ignore the fact that Luke's lips were now nuzzling at her ear. 'And the other mistakes?'

'The second is that they're not all beautiful—or not in the way you mean. If you look around you downstairs with your eyes instead of your prejudices you'll notice that the women here are as varied in age, weight and physical attributes as they are in race, colour or creed. We don't discriminate on *any* grounds—except skill at the job. The only thing they have in common is that they are all outgoing, extrovert, self-confident, irrepressible and generally sparky personalities—which just happens to be a pretty good recipe for attractiveness in a woman, as well as being the ideal make-up for sales.'

He stopped to draw breath. 'And your third mistake is to assume that I would risk my whole operation by sleeping with any one of them—no matter how attractive they might be.'

His new tone of seriousness gave her the courage to look round. 'Oh, come on, Luke,' she said sceptically. 'Are you telling me you've never been tempted? When you work with them all day?' It was Lexy's voice and imagined image that tormented her, though she couldn't bring herself to pronounce the name. It was obvious now that to most of these women Luke was nothing but a boss. If an attractive one. But Lexy had been something different. The only other 'A'. . .

But Luke's shrug seemed genuine enough. 'It would be fatal,' he said. 'A real harem must be hell to administer—even a working one is bad enough. A male boss working with this many women is walking a tightrope. I'd be a fool if I didn't realise that just being the boss invests me with a certain glamour, and it would be easy to let it slip out of control. Sales people are naturally competitive, but they've got to work as a team. Any sort of jealousy would crack the whole thing apart. So I make a joke of it—I flirt with everyone from the tea-lady to the sales manager and no one takes it seriously.'

'I see.' Suddenly, Folly felt absurdly happy. It was as if all the Wandas and Melissas of her imagination had just drifted ceilingwards with the steam. In fact, the heat was beginning to make her feel quite swimmy.

Unless it was the soft pressure of his lips as they nuzzled her throat. . .

'But fortunately you don't work for me,' he murmured. She could feel the words buzz through her flesh, starting at her neck and travelling downwards, until her whole body seemed to burn internally with a heat that could have flashed the water around them to steam. Except that the flame was deep inside, in a place that longed for him in a way she had never felt before.

'It took a lot to make me miss our date the other night, Folly,' he whispered. 'I know we haven't known each other long, but you've got under my skin like no other woman I've ever met. I can't stop thinking about you—I want you all the time. I want you to belong to me.'

His voice softened. 'I thought this could never happen to me—but now I know it already has. I love you, Folly—I think I've loved you all along. I was just too stubborn to realise it.'

'Oh, Luke. . .' There was a sensation like fireworks in her head as his words sank in. The miracle she had hoped for had happened at last. Luke Hunter had fallen in love.

But his voice pushed at her urgently, as if, having broken the barriers in his own mind, he needed to sweep her quickly towards a resolution. 'Folly, I don't want you to go on looking for a place of your own. I want you with me—all the time, not just an occasional evening. I want to look after you, my darling. I want——'

Folly felt her throat clench tight, suffocating her with anticipation. This was more than she had dared to hope. 'Oh, Luke. . .'

And then the tendrils of her inner fire licked outwards, and the buffeting of the waters around her merged dizzily with the touch of his hands as he drew her closer. And as they moved together Folly felt her lips part to welcome the hungry passion of his mouth.

Then the molten core seemed to burst its bounds, flooding her with its heat. And she felt herself spiralling down into the fiery darkness.

CHAPTER TEN

WHEN Folly came round, it was to feel herself tucked between cool sheets, and to see Luke's concerned face looking down at her. 'Are you all right?' he asked anxiously. 'The jacuzzi can be rather too much of a good thing if you're not used to it.'

And so can you, thought Folly dreamily. 'I'm fine,' she said out loud. Then, with sudden concern, 'Luke—I wasn't dreaming, was I? You really did say. . .' Her voice trailed off. Suddenly, it seemed utterly unbelievable, a mere figment of her dreamlike state.

But Luke's grin reassured her. 'Don't worry, Folly. I really did say it. I find it hard to believe it myself, but there it is. I love you, Aphrosyne Taylor-Agathangelou. And I don't intend to let you go.'

He bent down to kiss her on the lips, and Folly felt her head start to swim again as she reached up to place her hand behind his neck, drawing him down. But he disengaged himself gently and shook his head. 'Don't tempt me,' he said ruefully. 'It's almost lunchtime, and I have to be there. Duty calls. But I could have them send up a tray if you'd rather stay in bed.'

'No—I'll come down.' Folly sat up; then clutched the sheet to her as she realised with a shock that she was naked. She felt her face colour. 'Luke. . .? Did you. . .?'

He didn't pretend not to understand. 'That's my bed, woman,' he grinned unrepentantly. 'I was hardly going to leave you in your wet swimsuit. And besides—you were quite safe. I generally prefer my women conscious. Though I must admit,' he added musingly, 'you were a lot less trouble like that. . .'

'Pig!' Folly grabbed a pillow from behind her and threw it at Luke, then saw his face change with sudden desire as the sheet slipped down to expose her breasts.

'Oh, God, Folly. . .' he breathed. 'I want you so much. For two pins I'd send this lot home and have you all to myself.'

His eyes glinted gold as they devoured her. But the heady excitement Folly was feeling left no room for shame. 'Go on downstairs,' she said huskily. 'I'll join you when I'm dressed.'

He hesitated for a moment, then walked swiftly to the door. Folly watched him go. And as the door closed behind him she felt a surging wave of triumph. Luke wanted her—he loved her. As she loved him. He wanted to marry her. And the ghosts of Cherith and the others were banished for ever.

Lunch was served in a banqueting hall of extravagant dimensions and grandeur, and Folly ate ravenously, suddenly aware that she had eaten nothing since her lunch the day before. No wonder she had made such a fool of herself by fainting in the middle of Luke's proposal.

Both the food and the surroundings more than lived up to Luke's predictions. But to her disappointment there was no chance to talk privately with Luke himself. The conversation was, not surprisingly, centred around the work of the conference, and the language of 'prospects' and 'closures' left Folly feeling at sea.

Expecting more of the same, she wasn't looking forward to the seminar that followed. But Luke turned out to have the rare gift of making his subject not merely comprehensible, but absorbingly interesting.

His presentation methods were good too, using a mixture of direct lecturing, video, and taped examples to make his points.

The tapes came as something of a shock. Although several of them had been made by Luke himself, some of the others featured the voice that had caused Folly so much unnecessary grief.

'Sexy' Lexy's voice. Listening to them, Folly realised that she had never got around to asking Luke what he had been doing at Lexy's flat the night before. Now, she decided, it would be impossible to pose the question. It would only make Luke think that she was distrusting him again.

And besides, if there was one thing the last two days had taught her, it was that even the most suspicious circumstances could have perfectly innocent explanations. In this case, she could think of plenty herself. If she happened to bump into Lexy one day, it would do no harm to relieve her curiosity by some subtle questioning, but she had already established, by listening at the dinner table, that her supposed 'rival' was not among those present.

Turning to the woman next to her, she whispered, 'Where is Lexy, by the way? Why isn't she here?'

But the woman looked surprised. 'Oh, but she is. Didn't you know? But she came down with this dreadful flu bug, so she's taken to her bed.'

So Lexy was one of the three girls mentioned by the whispering woman who had shown her into the Seraglio. Folly realised virtuously that she could even feel sorry for her 'rival'. Then she turned her attention back to Luke's lecture, confident that she could now listen to the once-hated voice without a pang.

After the lecture was over, groups were formed to try out some of the techniques Luke had discussed.

And, to Folly's surprise and delight, he seemed to have planned his examples with her in mind. Although there was no direct reference to the Rose Bowl, Folly found herself part of a group discussing the hypothetical marketing problems of a small floristry business.

On the way out of the seminar-room, she managed to squeeze across to walk beside Luke.

'Thank you,' she said. 'I enjoyed that.'

'Did you find it useful?'

The adrenalin was still coursing through her veins. 'Oh, yes! It's given me loads of ideas, Luke—especially that "office plant-care" thing that we came up with. In fact, I was thinking I might try and start something along those lines as soon as I can. I thought I could put Lisa in charge of the maintenance side.' The words seemed to trip over each other in her enthusiasm. 'She comes across as lazy, but I'm sure it's just because Miss Philimore won't give her any responsibility. This could be just the job for her—and it would generate some new income to replace what we've lost. The only trouble is that it would really need some investment.'

A thought suddenly struck her, and she looked up at him uncertainly. 'Luke—does your offer still hold? About putting some money into the shop? Because if it does I might consider it now. . .'

She stopped, suddenly realising that she was letting her ideas run away with her. 'Well, we can talk about that later. But what do you think, Luke? Will it work?'

The smile he gave in reply sent the blood rushing to her cheeks. 'If you put as much into running it as you do into describing it, you'll have a good chance. So you're glad I brought you down here?'

Folly nodded. 'Though why you couldn't just have told me. . .'

He laughed. 'You deserved a lesson—and I doubt if

I could have talked you into it in any case. Would you ever really have believed me about my 'harem' if you hadn't met them?'

The two of them had slowed almost to a stop, and the other delegates were streaming past them towards the relaxation of the Seraglio. In a few moments they were alone.

'Perhaps not,' she admitted. And then, with difficulty, 'But why did you care? Why go to all this trouble for me, Luke, when I didn't even trust you?'

He touched her cheek. 'You know the answer to that one, Folly. And besides. . .' He paused for a moment, teasing her. 'I wanted to spend some time with you, and I rather doubted if you'd be susceptible to an offer of a weekend in Paris. So I thought I'd lull you into a false sense of security by luring you here.'

'A false sense of security? You mean, I'm still in danger?'

'Most definitely.' Luke grinned again; that wolfish grin she was coming to recognise. But her instincts no longer warned her to escape the hunter. From now on, any running she did would be into his arms.

He moved closer—and then a clock struck, somewhere in the distance, and he looked impatiently down at his watch.

'Damn. Look, Folly—I'm going to be pretty tied up for the rest of the day. But we need to talk—without you collapsing on me, flattering though that may be. Can I come to your room this evening? After dinner?'

Folly guessed from the timbre of his voice that he had more in mind than cool discussion. But the decision made itself, as if it had been made a long time before. 'Yes, Luke,' she whispered huskily. 'I'll be there.'

* * *

The dinner provided by the Seraglio's French chef was even more sumptuous than the lunch, but as a gastronomic experience it was wasted on Folly. She prodded at her *pâté de foie aux truffes de Perigord*, rearranged the *maigrets de canard* on her plate in the hope that she might be able to hide the tender slices of duck under her untouched vegetables, and, when the sweet trolley arrived, with its groaning layers of gâteaux and desserts, she mumbled an excuse to her neighbour and slipped away.

She didn't go back to her room. Luke, she knew, would be occupied for a long time yet, drinking coffee with the other women, talking over the day, helping to cement working relationships for the future. She managed to subdue the stab of jealousy that image brought. He was too much a professional to skimp such a vital part of the conference, no matter how pressing his personal motives might be.

And besides, she found herself glad of the breathing-space. Everything had happened so fast. She had gone from happiness to misery and back again in what seemed no more than hours, and the speed of the changes had left her with a sense of unreality that she found impossible to shake off.

She wandered out into the darkening grounds, across the lawn towards the trees. Everything that she had ever wanted was coming true. Luke loved her. He wanted to marry her; to be with her. And tonight they would seal that love together. Tonight. . .

The cool air caressed her bare arms, and Folly shivered and turned back towards the house. What did women do, who were waiting for their lovers? How could she sit calmly and read a magazine, when all the time she knew that any moment there would be a knock on the door, and Luke would be standing there, waiting? She started to wish that she had stayed at the table. At least then there would have been the chatter of her neighbours to distract her thoughts. Instead of this waiting. . .

But when she opened the door of her room he was waiting for her.

'Luke.'

He was sitting on the edge of the bed, his collar loosened and the tie he had worn at dinner hanging loose about his neck. His chin was shadowed and he looked tired. 'I thought for a moment that you'd run out on me.'

Folly shook her head. 'I thought you'd be longer. I just took a walk around the grounds.'

They were talking like strangers. She looked around for somewhere to sit, but the bed looked bigger than ever in the cramped room and his jacket lay discarded on the only chair.

She bent to pick it up, but his voice arrested her.

'Come here, Folly.'

She tried to move towards him. But something—the fear—held her back. 'I thought you wanted to talk.'

'I do. But that comes later, Folly. Don't be afraid.'

She walked the few steps towards him, her legs shaking like a toddler's, and stood in front of him, waiting. Her knees touched his and the tiny contact sent a quiver of anticipation up her spine. She could feel the hairs prickle on the back of her neck with the almost electrical charge.

'I'm not afraid.' As she said it, she knew it was true. This was where her life had been leading. . . And now she was here. 'Not really, Luke. Just nervous——'

'I know.' He drew her gently down until she was sitting sideways on his lap, then put his arms around to hold her gently, like a child. 'It's me who's scared. You terrify me, Folly. You make me feel—I don't know how you make me feel. But it's like nothing else I've ever felt before. You're so precious to me, Aphrosyne Taylor-Agathangelou. And I don't want to hurt you.'

'Oh, Luke. . .' Folly was suddenly filled with a shuddering sense of urgency. 'Oh, Luke, you won't hurt me.' She buried her face in his shoulder to hide her blushes. 'Make love to me, Luke,' she whispered. 'I want you so much. I need you——'

But her urgency seemed to provoke him to lazy slowness. 'Calm down, my impetuous little Aries. There's no need to rush. Loving was meant to be savoured—and we've got plenty of time.'

Their whole lives. . . 'I know. . .But oh—I want you, Luke. Oh, God—so much——'

'Come here, then.' With a long sigh he drew her close, his lips seeking hers. And as they met a passion exploded between them; a hunger that terrified Folly with its intensity. For a moment, she held back. And then his need called out an answering desire within her, and she found herself clinging to him with a desperation that matched his own.

The flame that had been burning inside her since their first kiss burst suddenly into flame. Fear, thought, will, regrets—everything fell before the conflagration like a forest in the fire. Folly hardly knew what she was doing. But no—that wasn't true. For the first time in her life, she knew exactly what she was doing, as her body and brain melted together in a harmony of desire.

All that was real was the pounding of her blood, and the hunger between them. His lips tore at hers, and hers at his, as if each one was the prey and each the hunter——

Luke rolled her back on the bed, their mouths still hungrily joined together, and she could feel his hand search behind her for the zip of her dress. She arched her back to aid him. And as the cold metal slid down her back, and the soft cloth fell loose around her shoulders, she felt a feeling of liberation so great that she wanted to cry out.

'Oh, Luke——'

With a groan, he pulled away, kneeling over her. One hand was tangled in her hair, holding her down, and with the other he traced a line past her collarbone and down on to the softer flesh beneath, tugging the neckline of her dress lower and lower, until Folly could feel it brush the swollen aureoles of her breasts under the silk of her bra.

Then, as if he had tormented himself beyond endurance, Luke ripped it clear, down past her waist and beyond. Folly gasped.

'I want to look at you. My God, you're beautiful.' His voice was hoarse, like a whisper, but it seemed to fill the room. He pulled again, and Folly raised her hips, arching wantonly towards him as the dress slipped past her hips. She felt it fall softly down her legs and to the floor.

Her body lay open before him, her only covering a few wisps of silk. Her breasts seemed to strain towards him, begging for his touch, and there was a wetness between her thighs that burned like fire.

Luke's eyes devoured her. 'Don't move.'

He stepped back off the bed and started to unbuckle his belt. Folly lay motionless, secretly revelling in her unaccustomed passivity, and watching him through half-closed eyes. He undid the buttons of his shirt and shrugged it from his shoulders, letting it fall unheeded to the floor. Then the zip of his trousers. . .

And all the time, his eyes never left her. They trailed across the plain of her stomach and the twin mounds of her breasts; glinting gold as they lingered on the silk between her thighs.

Her whole body was a pulse; throbbing; waiting. At last he was naked and she felt the rough touch of his skin slide over her, bearing her down. His chin grazed her navel as his lips traced the line of her belly, moving upwards to her breasts. And then his tongue——

'Oh!' A long animal cry was forced from her lips as his mouth teased her though the silk of her bra, the damp lace rough against her fired nerves. Her hands twisted in the coverlet beside her head, and she writhed in an agony of pleasure. Merciless, he lapped her, sucked her, grazed her with his teeth until the waves of sensation that beat against her were more than she could bear.

'Oh, God—no! Luke—no more. . .'

With a groan that seemed to come from the bottom of the earth, Luke reached down and tore away the lacy silk that covered her. Folly heard the fabric rip, and saw him cast it aside. 'I can't wait any longer, Folly. I've got to——'

'Oh, yes! I want you, Luke——'

His weight was on her now, the roughness of his thighs between her legs. Feverishly, Folly clutched at him, her arms twining around the broadness of his back; her fingers raking his flesh. She felt him nudge against her flesh, begging for entrance. And then, the plunging thrust that forced her, screaming, through the veils of pain and pleasure, filling her; completing her. She was borne on, helpless, by his male power.

And just at the point when she thought there was no more power of feeling in her, some deep instinct took over, and she found her body moving fervently with his rhythm. And she realised, at last, that the submission she had feared was not surrender, but release. And that in losing control she had gained something infinitely more precious... Something exploded inside her. And together they swept on remorseless, to the final crest.

Afterwards, she lay there, shattered, as if a long fall had dashed her body to the ground. Except that, instead of pain, her limbs were heavy with a sensual lassitude that drugged her senses. She couldn't move—would never move again. Would never want to...

Her head was cradled in the crook of Luke's left arm and she lay contentedly, feeling the rhythm of Luke's breathing beside her and watching the gentle rise and fall of his chest. His eyes were closed, and his face had a lazy, satisfied look. He was still a hunter—but one sated with his prey.

Folly drifted in and out of sleep, waking to find Luke's hand upon her breast and his eyes open, watching her.

'Happy?'

She could feel a joy greater than any she had known gently bubbling inside her. 'What do you think?'

'I think you're beautiful.' He ran one finger to the soft tip of her breast, touching it with infinite delicacy. 'No regrets?'

She shook her head. 'Oh, no. How could I? That was so lovely... And when we're married——'

But his whole body had stiffened beside her, and the hand on her breast clenched involuntarily, making her cry out with pain.

'Luke! What's the matter? Are you all right?'

'Oh, I'm all right,' he returned grimly. 'And my hearing is perfect. What are you talking about, Folly? I never mentioned marriage. And you know that as well as I do.'

He swung his legs over the side of the bed and stood up abruptly, reaching for his clothes. His dark figure stood between Folly and the light, seeming to tower above her, threatening.

She shook her head, as if this new and terrifying development might be a mere disorder of her brain. 'But you asked me, Luke. You asked me to marry you. That's why I——' She stopped, her face flooded with red. Would she really have refused him, if his proposal had never been made?

But that was irrelevant now. Made it certainly had been, and there was no way Luke could have forgotten it.

But it seemed he had. 'What the hell do you mean, I asked you to marry me? Do you think I wouldn't remember? I told you I loved you—I was even fool enough to ask you to move in with me. I naïvely thought that we had something special going for us. But now you tell me that the only reason you went to bed with me was because you thought you could up the stakes to marriage.'

He pulled on his shirt with such violence that a button sprang off and skittered across the floor. 'And my God! I suppose that's why you were suddenly in favour of my investing in the Rose Bowl. I suppose you thought that, if we were married, you wouldn't lose control...Well, I'm sorry to disappoint you, you ambitious little fool. But I told you once what my views were on marriage. And you overestimate your charms if you think one roll in the hay will make me change my mind.'

The deliberate cruelty of his words cut Folly like a knife. 'That's not true! Luke, I thought—I genuinely thought that was what you were asking me.' Desperately she searched her memory for his exact words, but they had drifted away like the steam that had stolen her senses. 'You said. . .you said you wanted to be with me. . .to live with me. . .You said you loved me. . . I was only half conscious, Luke. I must have assumed——'

'You assumed too much.' But his voice was calmer now, despite its rough edge. 'Are you seriously telling me that you thought I proposed to you this morning? In that damn bath?'

She nodded. 'I swear it, Luke.'

'And that, if you hadn't thought that, none of this——' he leaned over and touched her breast, giving a bitter laugh as the nipple sprang to immediate attention '—would ever have happened?'

She looked at him, not knowing what to say. 'How can I answer that?' she said at last. Some instinct told her that only the truth could save them now; that the time for evasions was over. But what was the truth? 'I've been in love with you ever since we met. You know that.'

She hesitated, then forced herself to carry on. 'You know what you do to me. What we had together wasn't faked. But if you're asking me whether I would have agreed to live with you, if I'd known that was what you were asking, I just don't know.'

'And what about the Rose Bowl? Would you have asked for my investment if you hadn't convinced yourself we were going to get married?'

But again her answer was the same. 'I don't know, Luke. Marriage would make a difference; you must see that.'

There was a long silence. Then, at last, Luke broke it. 'All right, then, you don't know. But there's an easy way to find out. I'm asking you now. Move in with me. You say you love me, Folly, whatever you mean by that. And you know damn well I care for you. So here's your chance. Let me be your lover.'

He shrugged, the jerky movement betraying for a moment the emotion he had banished from his voice. 'Maybe we'll still be together in five or ten or fifty years, or maybe not. There are no guarantees in this life; not even in marriage. Or haven't you looked at the divorce statistics recently? I'm offering you everything I can, Folly; and it's a damn sight more than I ever thought I'd offer any woman. The only difference is that I won't make promises that I can't keep.'

The seconds ticked away. Folly stared unseeing at the crumpled sheets, as if the bed that had so recently harboured their ecstasy might now prove the anodyne to pain. But there was nothing there to soften the agony of her decision.

What he said was true. She knew that marriage could never promise permanence. But something in her rebelled at Luke's stark acceptance of the risk. What chance could their love have when he so clearly saw it as something fragile, ephemeral?

'Luke,' she said abruptly, 'if I moved in with you, would you send me roses? I told you once they were my favourite flowers.'

She didn't know where the question had come from. But Luke only nodded, as if it made perfect sense. 'Roses are just another promise,' he said bleakly. 'I can't give you what you're asking, Folly. But there are other flowers.'

'Not for me.' Folly looked up at him sadly. He seemed a long way off. But now the truth was very clear. What she wanted from Luke Hunter was not a few months'—or even a few years'—sensual companionship. She wanted a lifetime's.

She wanted roses. And she could never settle for less.

CHAPTER ELEVEN

How long Folly sat there, she wasn't sure. Slowly, the tears dried up, and all that was left was the sense of emptiness. Of loss. And something else. An insidious voice that whispered in her head, '*You fool...*'

'There was nothing else I could do...' But even when she whispered them aloud the words had a hollow ring. Right or wrong, the result was the same. She had lost the one man she loved in all the world. No, worse than that—she hadn't 'lost' him. She had sent him away. And now she no longer had even the conviction of her rightness to sustain her.

Because the voice might be right. The more she thought about it, the more she realised that, as usual, she had let her actions rush ahead faster than her mind could follow. She had demanded commitment from Luke—the one thing she knew he wouldn't grant. But she herself had offered nothing in exchange.

No love, except for the clinging love he feared. No trust. Nothing of herself. She had stood there like a damsel in a high tower, imprisoned by her own fears, and had said imperiously, 'Here I am. Come to me.'

But, in the story, Rapunzel had let down her hair as a living rope to draw her beloved to her. She had risked—and suffered. But she had won her bridegroom.

Folly remembered again the passion they had shared. There had been more than just desire there, she had known it. There had been caring. There had been love. But she had turned away from her high window and demanded he scale the ivory walls without her help.

So he had turned and walked away. And she had done nothing to stop him.

'Oh, Luke,' she moaned. 'I want you so much. . .'

And the voice in her head whispered back.

'*How much*?'

Folly felt a stirring in the pit of her stomach, a quiver in the emptiness of despair. It was no comfortable emotion that pierced the veil, but even pain and fear were better than the emptiness that had preceded them. She forced herself to look at them; let them surround her. The pain of loneliness; the fear of betrayal. Fear of losing the man she loved best in the world. All the terrors that Tony had taught her came crowding back.

But the irony was that she had lost Luke already. And the fact that she had sent him away before he'd had time to betray her was cold comfort, set against the enormity of that loss. One by one, she felt her certainties crumble to dust.

It left her naked, and terrifyingly vulnerable. But almost at once she felt a thrill of excitement. There was still hope, after all. She could go to him—now; tonight. She could shut her eyes to the future and be content to share the present with him, as her body longed to do. Luke had already admitted that he loved her. And, in the end, she might not lose him after all. . .

And even if she did, she thought bleakly, could that grief be any worse than the pain she was already feeling? A possibility of future heartbreak against the certainty of present pain. . . It seemed like a fair exchange. If she could only find the courage to follow it through. . .But here, her resolution nearly failed her. She tried to imagine herself walking along the corridor, knocking on Luke's bedroom door and saying—saying what?

I was wrong, Luke—I want you, on any terms... Take me to bed, Luke... As the words formed themselves in her mind, she didn't know how she could ever utter them. Perhaps she wouldn't have to speak at all. But no, she would have to say something. What if he didn't understand?

She sat down in front of the mirror and brushed her hair carefully, as if the success of her enterprise lay entirely in the sleek disposal of each gleaming black thread. Luke's stamp lay on her; in the swollen fullness of her lips and the unnatural brightness of her eyes. Her olive skin glowed in the artificial light, the curves of her naked breasts softened into a newly voluptuous sensuality that reflected and heightened her resolution.

I am a woman... As she stared entranced at her own image, Folly felt a warming in her cheeks, and watched as a flush spread down from face to neck to breasts, dying the tender peaks a deeper hue. She felt the nipples stiffen, coiling the spring of desire tighter inside her. Then, with sudden resolution, she stood up.

She had spent her life rushing into things—and this was no time to stop. Her foolhardy Aries courage might be all that stood between her and a lifetime of misery. What did it matter that she didn't know what to say to him? When she saw him, the words would come.

Folly reached for the towelling bathrobe that hung behind the door, and made her way out into the corridor. Towards Luke Hunter's room.

She didn't hear the murmur until she was standing right outside the door to Luke's private apartment. She stopped, with her hand raised to knock. The sound came again, now quite plainly a man's voice. And, although the words were still indistinguishable, there was no doubt that it came from within.

Folly hesitated. She didn't want to complicate matters by disturbing Luke in the middle of a telephone conversation—or, worse still, a face-to-face discussion with one of his staff.

She glanced at her watch and saw that it was almost midnight. Surely no one would need to consult him at this hour? But on the other hand she couldn't stand out in the corridor indefinitely. She was already beginning to feel uncomfortably conspicuous.

Just as she was beginning to lose her courage, Luke's voice stopped, and she breathed a sigh of relief. At last! Her hand went back up to tap upon the door.

And froze, as another voice took over. Again, the words were indistinct, but the tone and quality were unmistakable.

All the blood drained from Folly's face as she listened, straining for the meaning that eluded her ears, and yet at the same time knowing that there could be no innocent explanation. Not of that voice, at that time and in that place.

Because from the very first syllable she had recognised it—even through the door. She had heard it before—not often, but always with Luke. It was Sexy Lexy's voice. . .No wonder Luke had suggested he come to her room earlier, rather than she go to his. And no wonder that, when she had rejected him, he hadn't bothered to argue. Why should he bother, when he had a willing partner waiting back in his rooms?

In her state almost of shock, Folly found her mind occupied with trivialities. Hadn't they said she had flu? But Luke's room was hardly a place to convalesce.

Desperately she sought for excuses when she knew

there was none. Perhaps Lexy had pretended illness to avoid meeting her; then let herself into Luke's room uninvited. She might have found herself unexpectedly welcome when he had returned, furious, from her own rejection. It would be some comfort to believe that Luke had turned to his old mistress only as second-best...Or perhaps——

But, whatever the chain of events that had led up to it, the result was the same. Luke and the mysterious Lexy were in there together... And, with a horrified shudder, it occurred to Folly that if she stayed any longer in the corridor she might hear more than talking in the room beyond the door.

That would be the ultimate betrayal—but it was one she didn't need to suffer. Her hand recoiled from the wooden panel as if it were red-hot, and she backed silently away. Her body felt stiff and awkward, as if the cold she felt had been physical enough to stiffen her muscles, as well as freeze her heart.

But at last she was back in her room, and sinking back against the closed door in a grief that was too deep for tears. And in the storm of emotion that threatened to overwhelm her there was only room for one thought.

That, whatever happened, she must not see Luke Hunter again—and certainly not here, on his own territory. Eventually she might have to face him as a customer, across the counter of the shop. But not yet—not until she had had time to rebuild her shattered defences.

She had to leave the Seraglio. And she had to leave tonight.

It was hardly the joyful mood in which Folly had expected to take possession of her new domain, but it seemed to work well enough. When Monday came, her misery gave her a new edge of ruthless efficiency, so that she hardly hesitated in rejecting some of the more out-of-condition stock that the retiring owner tried to include in the valuation. The stock-check and handover were finished in record time.

At last, Miss Philimore had departed, leaving Folly and Lisa alone. The next two hours were hectic, the Rose Bowl's new owner struggling alone with the lunchtime rush while her assistant made up the orders that should have been done earlier.

At first Folly had thought of reversing the roles, nervously picturing the arrival of a furious Luke, and the subsequent scene. But as she opened her mouth to suggest it, she gave herself a mental shake. She would not be reduced to skulking in the back room of her own shop. She was now the proprietress of the Rose Bowl. And if her duties included serving Luke Hunter, then she would manage it. Somehow. And without giving him the satisfaction of knowing how deeply he had hurt her.

But as the rush died down it became apparent that her resolute determination would not be needed. No tall figure loomed over the till as she was serving, or appeared suddenly from behind the window displays. Folly bit back the feeling of disappointment that crept over her, and summoned Lisa for a council of war.

'I don't know if you realise it, Lisa, but the Rose Bowl is in trouble,' she started bluntly. 'I didn't find out until after I'd taken the lease on, but the department store on the corner has taken a lot of our casual trade.'

Lisa looked a little guilty. 'I did wonder...' she said. 'When you first came in to look around I half thought I ought to mention it. We didn't get half the custom after they got revamped. But the old bat was always hanging around—and then the next thing I knew she was telling me you'd signed the lease. So I thought you must know what you were doing.'

Folly smiled ruefully. 'Knowing what I'm doing is something I'm better at in retrospect,' she admitted. Lisa would never know how true that was—or how nearly it had come to blighting her life. 'And I was pretty naïve. But don't blame yourself—you couldn't have been expected to warn me and risk your own job. I only mentioned it because I want you to know that I realise the problems we're facing—and that I've got plans to put us back on our feet. But I can't do it on my own. I'd like to feel that I can rely on you for help.'

The other girl seemed taken aback—but enthusiastic, lifting Folly's spirits a fraction at this confirmation of her judgement. 'What are you planning to do, then—renovate the place? I wouldn't have thought you could have afforded it so soon. What will you do? Get a loan from the bank?'

Folly shook her head, trying resolutely not to think of what might have been. 'No—you were right,' she sighed. 'I can't afford to take on a loan at this stage. Especially as there's no guarantee I won't fail. But in any case, I don't believe a face-lift is what we need. We need something more radical. . .'

Despite the misery that still numbed her emotions, Folly felt a trace of her former enthusiasm as she outlined the scheme, suitably cut down to take account of her lack of capital. At least some good had come out of her association with Luke. Without his help, she knew that the Rose Bowl would almost certainly have been doomed.

'We're not going to get back the passing trade,' she explained. 'That's gone forever. This simply isn't the right site to catch the Oxford Street shoppers. No, what we need is to take advantage of what is right outside our door.'

Lisa peered past the window display, as if half expecting to see a crocodile of new customers filing towards the door. 'What, concrete, you mean? Or skyscrapers?'

Folly found herself almost smiling. 'That's exactly what I do mean. Offices! We're already dabbling our toes in the market, with the account customers like L—— like Mr Hunter. But we could do far more. I want to start providing a complete office environment service—you know; pot plants, palm-trees, the lot. And we'd do the maintenance and watering instead of just selling the plants, which would give us a nice steady income. I thought you could take charge of that.'

'Me?' The awed pleasure in Lisa's voice spoke volumes. 'But what about the floristry side? Surely you wouldn't give that up altogether?'

'Oh, no!' Was this really the girl who had thought it all so 'boring' a few weeks earlier? 'Quite the opposite, really,' she went on. 'But what I would do is try and make it more popular, with special promotions and so on. Most of our potential customers are quite young—secretaries and office staff. They probably never even think of buying flowers for themselves. But if we could think up some really punchy window displays to tempt them in. . .'

She saw that this had really caught the other girl's imagination, and hurried to strike while the iron was hot. 'I thought you might have some good ideas for that as well, Lisa. After all, you're more the age we've got to go for. So perhaps you could give it some thought. . .'

They spent the rest of the afternoon in animated discussion—so animated that Folly had gently to point out to her employee that it was time to lock up. For once, the girl seemed genuinely sorry to be finishing work.

'We'll make a go of it, see if we don't,' she said to Folly as she left. 'You can't fail now—I want to keep this job. After six months working for old Philly I think I deserve a bit of luck!'

They laughed together, and as she locked up behind the girl Folly couldn't help realising that that was something else she owed Luke, however indirectly. If his betrayal hadn't led to her breaking down in Lisa's presence, she might never have discovered her assistant's unexpected resources. The thought dampened her mood, and, after turning the lights out, she sat in the dimness for a few moments, collecting her thoughts.

What she found hardest to forgive was not that Luke had betrayed her. It was that he had made her betray herself. If he hadn't been so hasty in consoling himself with Lexy, she would have rushed ahead with her usual blind enthusiasm, forgetting all the lessons her broken engagement had taught her. She would have given herself to a man for whom she was nothing but another short-term conquest, and in a year, or six months, or however long it took him to tire of her, she would have found herself alone again.

As she was now. And the worst betrayal of all was the fact that, even as she sat there, she was wishing she had had those few short months. . .

CHAPTER TWELVE

BEFORE Folly could give way to the tears that threatened her, a commotion on the road outside broke through her melancholy. A large delivery van was almost blocking the narrow street, its high sides nearly shutting off the daylight from her windows.

She stood up in annoyance. Surely he couldn't be intending to stop there? And then she saw to her amazement that the man who had just climbed down from the cab was knocking on her door.

'Yes?' she said ungraciously, unlocking it. 'I think you may have made a mistake. I'm not expecting any deliveries.'

The man consulted his delivery sheet. 'Miss Taylor? The Rose Bowl?'

'That's right. . . But I'm still not expecting anything.' Folly racked her brains, but she was sure there was nothing she had forgotten. 'What is it? And who is it from?'

'Flowers, love. This is a flower shop, isn't it? From a party called. . .' He consulted the paper again, and, after some hesitation, made out the name of the Rose Bowl's usual wholesaler. 'You want it brought in, or left on the pavement? I haven't got all night.'

Folly was still confused, but at least there now seemed to be light at the end of the tunnel. Presumably Miss Philimore had placed some sort of order before she left, forgetting that she would no longer be around to take delivery. Or maybe not forgetting. It would have been just like her to take a method like this to exact a petty revenge for their disagreements, landing Folly with a pile of unwanted stock that she couldn't refuse without souring relations with her supplier.

'Well, I didn't order them,' she said suspiciously. 'And I'm not paying for them if they're not what I want. Can I see the list?' The situation might be salvageable. She would need stock, after all, and if the selection wasn't too impossible she could probably keep it long enough to clear it. There was no point causing trouble if she could avoid it.

But the van driver was already round at the back of his vehicle, unloading boxes. 'There ain't no list, lady,' he said as he pushed past her with the first of the consignment. 'And there ain't nothing to pay. This little lot's already been taken care of.' He reappeared with another box, identical to the first. 'So how's about moving over and letting me get on with it, eh? Then we can both get home.'

Too taken aback to know what else to do, Folly stood aside and watched as he carried in four more boxes. The pile in the centre of the shop was now almost head-height, and he started another beside it.

Two more boxes. That made eight. 'What do you mean, there's no list?' she managed at last. 'There must be something. What does it say on your delivery sheet?'

'Look, lady, give me a break. I just deliver the stuff, I don't interview it for the Sunday papers.' He waved the paper at her, and, even at a distance, she could see that it said very little. 'Ten boxes, flowers, perishable, all paid up. To be delivered to the Rose Bowl. Which is here.' He stalked back out and came back in with two more boxes to dump down heavily with the others.

'Which I done,' he added flatly. 'So if you'll just give me a signature on this. . .'

Realising that there was nothing more she could get out of him, Folly signed mechanically, and the man gave an exaggerated sigh of relief. After he had gone, she stared blankly at the stack of boxes he had left.

It was all most irregular. For a start, she had definitely got the impression that Miss Philimore always did her buying in person. And even if she had decided to use a delivery service, there would normally be a full check-list to be ticked off before parting with any money. Otherwise how could the customer know she had got what she paid for?

And just what had been paid for in this case? Folly cut the tape that sealed the box nearest to her and pulled off the lid. Roses—a rich peach shade with a good strong scent. Well, that was a good start—they wouldn't be difficult to sell. But it made the mystery even deeper. Was it possible that the grasping Miss P had meant the gesture kindly? It seemed out of character—but then, facts were facts.

And roses were roses. The second box contained them too—red, this time. And the third. . . By the time she had opened all the boxes, the floor of the little shop was strewn with cardboard and tissue-paper, and the air was heavy with scent.

Folly knelt on the floor among the debris, her mind spinning with confusion. 'It doesn't make sense,' she whispered to herself. 'Who would send me all these roses?'

'I would.' The voice was unmistakable—except for its unaccustomed gentleness.

Folly froze. 'Luke——' Her ears full of the rustling of paper, she hadn't heard him approach. But he stood only feet away, towering above her. Folly found herself curiously reluctant to look up, as if by meeting his eye she might give him back the power he held over her.

But her gaze edged upwards, taking in the long, muscular legs and narrow hips, the broad chest in its businesslike white shirt. . .

'Folly.' The way he used her name seemed a statement rather than a question. It assumed so much—as if the link that was between them needed no words. . . And for a moment Folly was almost taken in by his quiet confidence.

Then the enormity of it hit her. How could he think—how could he possibly expect that this one dramatic gesture would wipe out all that had already passed between them? The memory came back to her of Lexy's low, sensual voice issuing from behind Luke's bedroom door, only hours after they had parted. How could he think she would forgive that?

And then she realised. Of course; he didn't know that she had stood there in the darkness and listened to the proofs of his betrayal. As far as Luke was concerned, she was still the naïve, trusting fool whom he had left to weep in her bedroom. And no doubt now he expected her to be suitably softened up by her two days' grieving, ready to fall back into his arms on the strength of one calculated gesture.

'It won't work, Luke,' she said bluntly. Her defiance gave her the courage to lift her eyes to his for the first time, and she saw the surprise and sudden uncertainty that flashed across them. 'The roses were just a symbol. You can't buy me with a few armfuls of flowers.'

'I didn't think I could.' There was a quiet sincerity in his voice that would have been very convincing. Even armoured by her knowledge, Folly felt herself waver. 'I've been a fool,' he went on. 'But not that much of a fool. Not fool enough to stand aside and watch the best thing that's ever happened to me wither away because

I'm too scared to let it put down roots. I know what the roses mean. And I'm offering them to you.'

It was almost beyond belief. Everything she'd ever wanted laid temptingly before her—only she had looked behind the scenes and knew the display was a hollow sham. She felt a flame of anger flicker and grow. There was no point in stringing this out. All she wanted was for him to leave and take his tantalising, lying promises away with him.

'What's happened, then?' She let the contempt she felt twist her voice. 'Did Lexy turn you down?'

But if she had expected a reaction of guilty surprise she was disappointed. Luke just looked puzzled. 'What do you mean? What is all this about Lexy?' He laughed—actually laughed. 'Anyone would think you were jealous of the woman.'

The sound of his laughter fanned the flame of anger to new heights. Folly felt something burst inside her, and she no longer wanted just to escape Luke; she wanted to strike out at him; hurt him as he had hurt her. 'Oh, I'm not jealous,' she parried cruelly, standing upright to face him. 'That would imply I still wanted you, wouldn't it, Luke? But since I've realised just what a bastard you are I'm afraid I've rather lost interest. Lexy's welcome to you. I just hope she knows what she's getting.'

But the stroke made none of the impact she was expecting. Luke just looked more puzzled, reaching out to touch her as if to help him understand. 'But you can't be jealous.' He was still half laughing at her. 'Not of *Lexy*. Damn it, Folly, what is all this really about?'

His air of innocence was the last straw. Folly blew up. 'I'll tell you what it's about! It's about the fact that when you walked out and left me on Saturday night you went straight to Lexy! And there's no point lying about it. I was outside your bedroom that night—I heard you together. She's obviously prepared to put up with your terms. I'm not, and I never will be.'

'Go back to her...' Luke still sounded more mystified than angry or guilty. 'Folly, somehow we've managed to get a crossed line here. You can't possibly have got it into your head that I'm having some kind of affair with *Lexy*, of all people. I mean, I know these things are more common now, but there is the age difference for a start.'

'I don't see why that would stop you.' Folly remembered the young girl she had seen when delivering the flowers, and her obvious hero-worship of her boss. If Lexy was another like her it might explain why she was willing to accept such cavalier treatment. Luke's age would only add to his glamour. 'Presumably she's past the age of consent.'

'The age of consent?' Now Luke looked really bewildered. 'What the hell do you mean? You know how old Lexy is, for goodness' sake. You've met her. And, although I'm sure her husband loves her dearly, even he would have to admit that she's not exactly *femme fatale* material.'

'Her husband?' It was Folly's turn to be bewildered. 'And what do you mean, I've met her? I admit I came close, the night I delivered those flowers, but for some reason you didn't think to introduce us. She was upstairs, if you remember.' Luke might not, but Folly did, and the memory gave her back the edge of anger. 'In bed,' she almost spat. 'Waiting for you. Obviously the fact that your Sexy Lexy was married didn't trouble you then.'

Luke was still staring at her as if expecting a rabbit to emerge from her sleeve at any moment. 'I don't believe it,' he said at last, half to himself. 'I've never met a girl with such a talent for getting hold of the wrong end of any available stick. I'd swear you could do it with a child's hoop.'

It was obvious to Folly that he was playing for time. 'Luke, I don't think——'

'Good. I told you before that thinking doesn't seem to be your strong point. So why don't you try listening for a change?'

Folly opened her mouth to protest again, then subsided. She might as well let him get his excuses off his chest. This time, she was in no danger. The knowledge she had of him would armour her against belief.

Luke smiled a little grimly at her submission. 'That's better. Now let's take this point by point. Having reluctantly cleared me of the charge of indulging in orgies with my entire sales force, you seem to have got it into your head that Lexy and I are carrying on some kind of affair. Is that right?'

'Yes, and I——'

'I said listen, don't talk. Second point: although you obviously have such a low opinion of me that it doesn't strain your credulity to believe that I was making love to two women at once, one of them married, I can't believe that even you could see me in the role of toyboy. From which I deduce that you hadn't realised that Lexy is fifty-three next birthday. . .' He watched Folly's jaw drop open with malicious satisfaction. 'No, I thought not. But you have met her, you know. When we arrived at the Seraglio, it was Lexy Everard who showed you in.'

Folly remembered the grey-haired, motherly-looking woman whose whispering voice had confirmed her earlier misconceptions. She felt herself waver. But no, it didn't add up. 'I'm not quite as gullible as you seem to think, Luke,' she snapped. 'That can't be Lexy.

Quite apart from the fact that no one in their right mind would nickname that woman "Sexy", I would have recognised her voice. I'd heard it before, remember. And I heard it again in your room on Saturday night.'

'You said that before, and I didn't understand it then. Unless. . .' His face suddenly cleared. 'Folly, is there a Greek word that means utter, earth-shattering stupidity?'

His sudden change of direction confused her still further. '*Elithie*, I suppose. But why on earth——?'

'Because I may decide to re-christen you. If you remember, when you met Lexy she was going down with flu—her best friend wouldn't have recognised her voice. In fact, that's why I was at her house the night before. She started coming down with it when we were on our business trip, arranging this weekend. So I thought I'd better deliver her back to her husband. Who, I might add, was busy putting her to bed when I answered the door to you.'

Folly stared at him, all her suspicions re-aroused. She had been wrong; it was a mistake to listen to him. Luke Hunter could have talked his way out of the Tower of London. . .'In that case, what was she doing in your room the other night?'

Luke seemed vastly amused by the question. 'I might ask you, my young idiot, what you were doing listening at my door.'

She felt her face colour, but before she could invent an answer Luke had broken in again. 'I see,' he said slowly. The look of pleasure that glinted through his eyes convinced Folly that his guess was all too close to the mark. 'So you were coming to me. But you heard Sexy Lexy's voice. . . Incidentally, did you know who gave her that nickname originally?'

Folly shook her head impatiently. She neither knew nor cared.

But Luke seemed determined to tell her. 'It was one of her customers, in the days before I made her my manager,' he said lightly. 'One of her *telephone* customers. You're not the first person to be impressed by her voice. It made her very effective.' His own voice sounded rather odd, as if he was under strain. 'That's why I used her for so many of the taped examples for my lectures, Folly. Do you remember those tapes?'

'Of course I remember. Don't try and put me off, Luke. I want to know what she was doing in your—— Oh!' Her voice seemed to go very small. 'You mean, what I heard was the tapes?'

But, almost as if he hadn't heard her, Luke's voice carried on. 'When I left you that evening, my emotions were pretty churned up, Folly. I was furiously angry, and I needed desperately to believe it was with you. . . Anyway, I sat down and tried to put you right out of my head by immersing myself in work. Including going over the tapes for the next day's lectures.'

Almost the last brick in the wall of Folly's resistance had been demolished, but there was something that still rankled. 'But you gave her an "A", Luke,' she whispered. 'On the floristry books, she was an "A". The top category. She was the only one apart from me.'

He stared at her, and then his face crumpled into a smile. 'Oh, my poor Folly. . .We've been together for five years, Lexy and I—she practically holds that company together. Of course I gave her an "A". But that doesn't mean I'm having an affair with her.'

All Folly could think of was how near she had come to losing him. 'Oh, Luke. . .' she whispered. 'I've been such a fool.'

'Not as much of a fool as I tried to be. I thought I could work you out of my system, Folly. But you were far too deeply ingrained. By next morning I'd only got as far as realising that I had to talk you round.' He laughed shortly. 'Notice my arrogance. It hadn't occurred to me then that it might be me who was wrong. So anyway, I came looking for you. And found you gone.'

In those last few words, Folly could hear an anguish that matched her own. 'I got a taxi,' she explained, remembering the odd look the driver had given her when she had confessed she had no idea where she was and wanted to go all the way to London. 'It cost me a fortune—but I didn't think I could bear to see you again. If only I'd stayed——'

'Thank goodness you didn't.' Luke reached out and shook her gently by the shoulders. It was the first time he had touched her. 'It was thinking I'd lost you that brought me to my senses. I realised that I was still blaming you for what Cherith did to me. In some ways, you're very similar—oh, not in anything important. But she was ambitious, like you. And when you started to talk about marriage, it all seemed to be happening again. Especially since you'd just asked me about investing in your business. . .'

'Luke, I never cared about that. It was just a thought——'

But he shook his head. 'I know that, Folly. I'd talked myself into caring more for some worn-out principle than about the reality of what was happening to us. And as soon as I faced up to that, I realised my fears no longer applied.'

'What do you mean?' There was a hope springing inside her, but Folly scarcely dared to trust it. After all, she had been wrong about everything else.

'I mean that all my fears about marriage were based on my experience with Cherith.' He shrugged apologetically. 'Anyway, it suddenly became blindingly obvious that with you it would be different.'

'How different?'

He pulled her closer. 'I think you know. But, just to make sure you don't jump to any more ludicrous conclusions, I'd better make it clear that I don't ever intend you to get away from me. I love you, Folly. Which makes marriage seem the only sensible thing to do.'

But despite the happiness that surged within her at his words, Folly hesitated. He had been so sure before—and anything would be better than a decision that he might later come to regret. 'Oh, Luke, I love you too,' she whispered. 'But you don't have to do this. If you want, I'll live with you. I'll——'

But he stopped her stammering mouth with a kiss. And, gentle though it was, the touch of his lips held the seed in it of all the passion they had shared—and would share, she knew now, in the future. 'I know,' he murmured. 'You came to my room, remember? You were braver than I was, Folly. You were ready to give up what you believed in—and I couldn't even bring myself to abandon a few outworn prejudices.'

Relaxing against the comforting wall of his chest, Folly couldn't resist a little teasing. 'How do you know that was why I came to you? I might just have thought of some new names to call you.'

'I doubt if you could have thought of any I didn't deserve. If we'd been engaged, I might have thought you'd come to give me back my ring.' His bantering tone was as light as hers. 'But as we weren't. . .Which reminds me. . .'

He reached into his pocket and brought out a tiny

leather box. 'I wanted to give you a rose that wouldn't fade.'

Folly saw a glimpse of gold, and something that sparkled, then caught her breath as he slipped a narrow band on to the third finger of her left hand. 'Oh, Luke—it's beautiful.' The diamonds burned on her finger in a perfect rosette of white fire.

'Diamonds are the Aries birthstone—I looked it up. It seemed a good choice—they've got your sparkle.'

She couldn't take her eyes off it. 'And gold is the Leo metal, Luke,' she whispered. 'My sparkle and your strength—it makes a good combination, don't you think?'

'Then you will wear it for me?'

Her heart was almost too full for speech. 'Oh, Luke, of course I will. I love you so much.' Then, basking in the look of adoration that rewarded her, she added teasingly, 'Does this mean that I'm now a fully paid up member of Hunter's Harem?'

'The one and only member,' he growled. 'Let's have no more nonsense about that. And if I catch you suspecting me of an affair with my housekeeper I'll——'

'You'll what?' Folly's voice was brightly innocent.

'I'll have to take you to bed and remind you what a harem's duties are. Not that I plan to give you time to forget.'

Folly found her eyes drifting provocatively towards the privacy of the workroom. 'I think my memory's a little hazy already.'

Luke's answering grin sent a warm flush of desire flooding through her. 'What about these flowers, my impulsive little Aries? After all the fuss you made about my giving you roses, shouldn't you put them in water first?' But his voice was husky, and she knew that his need and love were as urgent as hers.

She started towing him towards the back room. 'They'll wait,' she said confidently. 'I'm the expert, remember? And besides—I've got the most important one right here.'

She touched Luke's ring on her finger, and for a moment felt the tears burn at her eyes. But they were tears of happiness.

For he was right. This was one rose that would never fade. The flame that sparkled in its heart was the same fire that had flared between them since the beginning. Like their love, it would last forever. And she knew it would always be her favourite flower.

STARGAZING

YOUR STAR SIGN: **ARIES (March 21st–April 20th)**

ARIES is the first sign of the Zodiac, ruled by the planet Mars and controlled by the element of Fire. These make you hot-headed, proud, impetuous and—sometimes—selfish. Your high degree of motivation, optimism and ambition make you a natural leader and when something needs doing, you get down and do it—right through to the end!

Socially, Ariens are extrovert and enthusiastic—you possess an excellent sense of humour and a great zest for living generally. At home you are likely to be the head of your household, though your explosive temperament can mean a bumpy ride for those around you!

Your characteristics in love: Affectionate and generous, Ariens tend to fall in love at first sight and then put their partner on a pedestal, being ardent, loyal and even sentimental until they discover that he/she is human after all. None the less, you can be a very exciting lover and your optimism and outgoing nature will help you create a finely tuned, balanced relationship. For the Aries woman, relationships with the opposite sex can cause problems because you hate to take the submissive role; being so hot-headed and quick-tempered, you won't settle for second best. Therefore you are likely to opt for partners who are gentle, tactful and charming.

Star signs which are compatible with you: Leo, **Sagittarius**, **Gemini** and **Aquarius** are the most harmonious, while **Libra**, **Cancer** and **Capricorn** provide you with a challenge. Partners born under other signs can be compatible, depending on which planets reside in their Houses of Personality and Romance.

What is your star-career? Frequently capable of running half a dozen things at once and relishing lots of action, Aries is born with an intense drive to succeed and to rise to the top. Positions which involve a good degree of organisation or high-level management and mental challenge will appeal to you, such as military service, sales and marketing, medicine—especially surgery—sports, teaching, rescue services and the world of high finance.

Your colours and birthstones: ancient astrologers linked Aries to the red tint of Mars, which appeared in the sky during March and April: therefore, the fiery colours of scarlet and pink are right for you.

Your birthstones are bloodstone and diamond; bloodstones were used in the past to staunch wounds, and as an antidote to stress and aches and pains. Diamonds—as stones of total perfection—were a token of love. Worn on the left-hand side, they were said to give the wearer the strength and protection, and to drive away the devil.

ARIES ASTRO-FACTFILE

Day of the week: Tuesday.
Countries: England, Germany and Poland.
Flowers: geraniums, honeysuckle, sweetpea.
Food: Pineapple and onions; Ariens like cooking in front of guests and enjoy serving fondues, flambé dishes and barbecues—very appropriate for a Fire sign!
Health: be careful not to let frustration get the better of you—or you'll have cuts and bruises to prove it! Co-operation with others is your secret to good emotional and physical health.

You share your star sign with these famous names:

Warren Beatty
Marlon Brando
Elton John
Dirk Bogarde
Dudley Moore

Julie Christie
Diana Ross
Samantha Fox
Doris Day
Ali McGraw

Mills & Boon

Next month's Romances

Each month, you can choose from a world of variety in romance with Mills & Boon. These are the new titles to look out for next month.

DISHONOURABLE PROPOSAL Jacqueline Baird
MISTAKEN ADVERSARY Penny Jordan
NOT HIS KIND OF WOMAN Roberta Leigh
GUILTY Anne Mather
DELIBERATE PROVOCATION Emma Richmond
DEAREST TRAITOR Patricia Wilson
ISLAND PARADISE Barbara McMahon
SUMMER'S ECHO Lee Stafford
MY ONLY LOVE Lee Wilkinson
RAINBOW OF LOVE Kay Gregory
CIRCLES OF DECEIT Catherine O'Connor
LOVE ISLAND Sally Heywood
THE INTRUDER Miriam Macgregor
A HEART SET FREE Nicola West
RENT-A-BRIDE LTD Emma Goldrick
STARSIGN
FORGOTTEN FIRE Joanna Mansell

Available from Boots, Martins, John Menzies, W.H. Smith, most supermarkets and other paperback stockists.

Also available from Mills & Boon Reader Service, P.O. Box 236, Thornton Road, Croydon, Surrey CR9 3RU.

AN EXCITING NEW SERIAL BY ONE OF THE WORLD'S BESTSELLING WRITERS OF ROMANCE

BARBARY WHARF is an exciting 6 book mini-series set in the glamorous world of international journalism.

Powerful media tycoon Nick Caspian wants to take control of the Sentinel, an old and well established British newspaper group, but opposing him is equally determined Gina Tyrell, whose loyalty to the Sentinel and all it stands for is absolute.

The drama, passion and heartache that passes between Nick and Gina continues throughout the series - and in addition to this, each novel features a separate romance for you to enjoy.

Read all about Hazel and Piet's dramatic love affair in the first part of this exciting new serial.

BESIEGED

Available soon
Price: £2.99

Available from Boots, Martins, John Menzies, W.H. Smith, most supermarkets and other paperback stockists.
Also available from Mills & Boon Reader Service, PO Box 236, Thornton Road, Croydon, Surrey CR9 3RU.

ESCAPE TO THE RUGGED OUTBACK, EXPERIENCE THE GLAMOUR OF SYDNEY, AND RELAX ON A PARADISE ISLAND...

Four new Romances set in Australia for you to enjoy.

WILD TEMPTATION – Elizabeth Duke
WOMAN AT WILLAGONG CREEK – Jessica Hart
ASKING FOR TROUBLE – Miranda Lee
ISLAND OF DREAMS – Valerie Parv

Look out for these scintillating love stories from April 1992

Price: £6.40

Available from Boots, Martins, John Menzies, W.H. Smith, most supermarkets and other paperback stockists. Also available from Mills & Boon Reader Service, PO Box 236, Thornton Road, Croydon, Surrey CR9 3RU.

4 FREE

Romances
and 2 FREE gifts
just for you!

*You can enjoy all the
heartwarming emotion of true love for FREE!
Discover the heartbreak and the happiness, the emotion
and the tenderness of the modern relationships in
Mills & Boon Romances.*

*We'll send you 4 captivating Romances as a special offer
from Mills & Boon Reader Service, along with the chance to
have 6 Romances delivered to your door each month.*

Claim your FREE books and gifts overleaf...

An irresistible offer from Mills & Boon

Here's a personal invitation from Mills & Boon Reader Service, to become a regular reader of Romances. To welcome you, we'd like you to have 4 books, a CUDDLY TEDDY and a special MYSTERY GIFT absolutely FREE.

Then you could look forward each month to receiving 6 brand new Romances, delivered to your door, postage and packing free! Plus our free newsletter featuring author news, competitions, special offers and much more.

This invitation comes with no strings attached. You may cancel or suspend your subscription at any time, and still keep your free books and gifts.

It's so easy. Send no money now. Simply fill in the coupon below and post it to -
Reader Service, FREEPOST, PO Box 236, Croydon, Surrey CR9 9EL.

NO STAMP REQUIRED

Free Books Coupon

Yes! Please rush me my 4 free Romances and 2 free gifts! Please also reserve me a Reader Service subscription. If I decide to subscribe I can look forward to receiving 6 brand new Romances each month for just £9.60, postage and packing free. If I choose not to subscribe I shall write to you within 10 days - I can keep the books and gifts whatever I decide. I may cancel or suspend my subscription at any time. I am over 18 years of age.

Name Mrs/Miss/Ms/Mr _____ EP18R

Address _____

_____

Postcode_____ Signature _____

Offer expires 31st May 1992. The right is reserved to refuse an application and change the terms of this offer. Readers overseas and in Eire please send for details. Southern Africa write to Book Services International Ltd, P.O. Box 41654, Craighall, Transvaal 2024.
You may be mailed with offers from other reputable companies as a result of this application.
If you would prefer not to share in this opportunity, please tick box. ☐